THE ACCIDENTAL

A REDEMPTION INC. NOVELLA

LAYLA REYNE

The Accidental

Cover Design: Sleepy Fox Studio

Editing: Adam Mongaya, Lori Parks

E-Book ISBN: 978-1-962010-36-8

Paperback ISBN: 978-1-962010-37-5

Content Warnings: Explicit sex; explicit language; violence; discussion of off-page/past homophobia and transphobia.

ABOUT THIS BOOK

Chef February Winters hates Valentine's Day. She refuses to open her restaurant for it. Until the critics say that she *can't*, so of course she *must*. But planning the perfect V-day menu eludes her.

Jax Dillon is a hacker, but for the past three months they've been tending bar. And on the lookout for a rogue spy. Truth be told, they've spent more time looking at the stunning head chef.

Feb's been looking Jax's way too, and the two mix up a sublime V-day concept. But when the big day arrives, Feb finds her restaurant full of bounty hunters and assassins. And when the spy she thought was a critic takes her three stars—and Jax—hostage, Feb must cook the meal of her life to win back culinary glory and the bartender (er, hacker?) who's stolen her heart. Good thing she's a real chef.

The Accidental is a prequel novella in the Redemption Inc. series. This sapphic romantic suspense features a non-binary hacker and the grumpy rising-star chef who accidentally finds herself in love and in the espionage pressure cooker.

AUTHOR'S NOTE

The Accidental was previously published as *Under the Table*, as part of the Accidentally Undercover multi-author series. No substantive changes or additions have been made from the prior publication. It has been retitled, recovered, and rereleased as a prequel novella in the Redemption Inc. series.

PROLOGUE

February Winters.

As much as Feb loved her parents, she cursed them daily for that particular gift. According to them, it was in honor of her February fourteenth birthday. *Valentine*, they'd said, was too on the nose. And February wasn't? If she had to guess, her dad had caught a case of Captain Obvious from all that *John Madden Football* he'd played, and after thirty-six hours of labor, her mom had been too damn tired to care.

The name was hell as a kid, and it only got more hellish as she climbed the professional kitchen ladder. Food critics loved a punny headline, and February Winters was a picnic basket full of fucking eye rolls.

February is Not for Lovers.

WinterHell's Kitchen.

February's Cold Winter.

All because she refused to open Under the Table, her baby, a shining star of the San Francisco food scene, on Valentine's Day. Because she refused to serve some boring as fuck prix fixe menu like every restaurant was expected to do that one night a year when everyone took their sweetheart out for dinner.

One, she didn't do sweethearts.

Two, it was her birthday.

Three, it was everything Under the Table wasn't.

But this year . . . she decided to do it. On her terms.

Even a date with her maybe-sweetheart after.

Her terms, however, did not include hiding under the table at her restaurant by the same fucking name, but there she was.

Feb was not looking forward to tomorrow's punny headlines.

ONE

The week before . . .

Feb spun on the barstool in her chef's nook, flipping her pen around her thumb and watching through the interior glass window as her staff glided around the kitchen. No service tonight; just an afternoon of planning and mise en place for the week ahead. The music was turned up, the vibe relaxed, all smiles and shit talk, everyone productive without the stress of incoming tickets. Would the bomb Feb was about to drop destroy a perfectly good Monday?

A flash of icy blue drew Feb's gaze to her head bartender weaving through the rows of stations, sampling this or that bite the chefs offered. Dylan Jacks had joined them three months ago, and they'd spent more time in the kitchen than any bartender Feb had ever worked with. They didn't need to be at the restaurant more than a couple of hours each Monday. Just enough time to prep and stock the bar and let Feb know if they were running low on anything. But Dylan was usually there longer, spending extra time in the kitchen, chatting and tasting and taking notes on their personal tablet, and then like clockwork, the cocktail menu was updated every Tuesday to reflect the week's ingredients. Expertly so. All of Dylan's drinks were amazing, sophisticated but edgy, surprising yet comforting, and all exactly the vibe Feb wanted for Under the Table.

Exactly the vibe Feb would use to describe Dylan as well. Their mohawk defied gravity and had been candy-cane striped for the holidays before the pale wintery blue it was now. The tunnels and plugs in their ears were usually jeweled to match whatever lipstick Dylan wore that day. And their wardrobe straddled a seemingly impossible line —on off days and prior to service, they dressed the part of nerd in button-downs and funny ties, always with their tablet tucked under their arm, but behind the bar, they were the coolest person you'd ever meet in head-to-toe leather.

They'd once offered to dress more formally for service, but Feb had shot the suggestion down. Contradictions fascinated her. She'd decorated UTT's entire dining room with them, from the painted black cement floors and soft pewter walls, to the navy, magenta, and purple velvet booths and chairs, to the bright white shiplap roof that arched over the entire space. Dylan, an equally fascinating contradiction, fit right in behind the room's centerpiece, a bar made from the same live edge wood as the tables in the rest of the dining room. Together, the two—Dylan and the bar—had starred in more than a few of Feb's dreams lately.

But as Feb glanced again at her chef's notebook, at the blank page under the scribbled heading *V-day Menu*, she wondered if her obsession with contradictions had gone too far. Had her determination to be contrary outpaced the practical, at least where her culinary imagination was concerned? Because her subconscious sure as fuck hadn't provided any inspiration on the V-day menu since she'd decided to be, well, contradictory. Thankfully, she'd surrounded herself with chefs more talented than herself.

Drawing her phone out of her pocket, she opened the app that controlled the restaurant's music and lowered the kitchen volume. Heads swiveled in her direction as she slid off her stool, exited the nook, and came to stand in front of the expeditor's station. She tossed her notepad onto the slab of colorful mosaic tile she'd laid by hand, her own finishing touch made three years ago, finished barely in time to open the doors. She felt more nervous—more lost—now than she'd ever been then. "I don't know how to do this."

Her sous-chef, Adi, straightened from where she and Dylan were sampling a kohlrabi noodle bowl she'd been working on the past few days. "Do what?"

"A Valentine's Day menu."

Adi dropped her spoon, Dylan choked on their slurp of noodles, and more gasps echoed around the kitchen. At the pastry station in the cold nook, a surprised Lacey cursed and squeezed her piping bag so hard she drowned a cupcake in yuzu frosting. "We're working Valentine's Day?" she squeaked.

"If you've already made plans, keep them." This was the third V-day since UTT had opened, and Feb had been staunchly opposed the past two years. If she opened without a prix fixe, she'd catch hell from the special occasion diners who managed to snag a reso, only to balk at the price tag and too adventurous ingredient list. If she opened with a prix fixe, her conscience would revolt, and their regular clientele would whisper she was selling out. Damned if she did, damned if she didn't, so for the past two years, she'd noped out altogether. Her staff had no reason to think this year would be any different. Hell, she'd said as much when Dylan had asked her about it last week. Feb wouldn't penalize Lacey or anyone for their absence on what was typically a night off; she wouldn't say no to any extra hands, though. "But if you're available that night, yes, we're going to open, and I could use your help. Assuming I can sort a menu."

"Well," Juan said from his sauce station, "what do you love about Valentine's Day?"

"Nothing."

"About romance?" Chloe asked as she slid a bowl of roasted chickpeas onto the tiles beside Feb's notepad.

"I've had two relationships. Both went about like hollandaise. Pretty for a hot minute before it breaks." She tossed a few of the crunchy chickpeas into her mouth and delighted at the pop of flavor on her tongue, smoky heat from the ancho chili powder but with a touch of spicy brightness on the finish. "These are excellent, Clo. The sumac is a nice touch."

"Thank you, chef."

"Isn't your birthday on Valentine's Day?" Adi asked.

"Let me tell you how much fun *that* was growing up. The amount of pink stuffed toys I received from relatives . . ." She rolled her eyes with a groan, then gestured at herself. "Have you ever seen me wear a scrap of pink?" Black constituted ninety percent of her wardrobe, the other ten percent blues and grays. Even UTT's chefs' coats were black.

"What did you do with them?" Juan asked. "All the pink toys?"

"Sent them with my mom to the animal hospital."

Adi served up an "Aww" with a heaping side of sarcasm, and Feb flicked a chickpea at her for the sass.

Everyone laughed, including Dylan, who strolled across the kitchen to the opposite side of the expeditor's station. They gestured at the notepad. "May I?" At Feb's nod, Dylan picked up the pad and pen. "What do you hate about Valentine's Day?"

"Pink."

More laughter, but all of Feb's attention was riveted on the upturned corners of Dylan's plum-painted lips. She idly wondered if they were soft and if they tasted like plum too. "Okay, what else?" Dylan asked.

"What else what?"

Dylan smirked, hitching that smile higher. "Valentine's Day. The bad."

Blinking, she wrenched her attention from Dylan's lips and met their gaze as she began ticking off "the bad" on her fingers. "It's so commercialized. It makes people believe that's the only night someone deserves to feel special. It makes people without partners feel not special. And it makes aromantic and some ace folks feel wrong."

The kitchen went silent, Dylan scratching notes on the pad the only sound in the rarely so quiet space. After another moment, Dylan laid down the pen and handed the pad to Feb.

Solo resos. Local ingredients. No pink.

Feb glanced back up, her lips lifting to match Dylan's smug smile. "I like it." She slapped the notepad against her palm, then addressed her chefs. "We only do solo reservations, we use local ingredients, and nothing remotely pink leaves this kitchen."

"I like it too," Adi said with a nod, then spun on her

heel and clapped her hands. "All right, let's get to work. Contest kitchen. Dishes in forty-five."

Dylan's eyes grew wide as chaos erupted around them, chefs running between stations, the pantry, and the fridges. Chuckling, Feb pulled Dylan to her side of the station before they got run over. "Adi is a food competition junkie," she explained. "Whenever we need to conceptualize something, she goes into contest mode. It usually produces spectacular results, so I've got no qualms with it. In fact"—she handed the pad back to Dylan—"I might get in on this one. I've got an idea."

"I can't wait to taste it." The heat in their sparkling green eyes sent Feb's mind racing a different direction, fantasies unspooling of the bar, Dylan, and what else they could taste. Dylan's next words unraveled more. "I'll also toss that bottle of pink hair dye I bought yesterday."

Now that was something pink Feb would love to see—the ultimate contradiction. She lifted a hand to push back a strand of Dylan's mohawk that had fallen forward but caught herself at the last second. By the flare of fire in Dylan's gaze, she was pretty sure the contact would be welcome, but she was also pretty sure she shouldn't be doing so here, in front of the rest of the staff. "I like it this frosty blue," she said, lowering her hand to rest next to Dylan's on the tiles, their fingers brushing. "But I think if anyone is edgy enough to temper some pink, it'd be you."

Dylan's fiery gaze melted into something darker and more elemental. "Not sure temper is the word you're looking for."

———

Each week at the restaurant had a natural, familiar rhythm to it. Monday planning and prep, then a steady ramp-up to the weekend rush. This Thursday, though, felt more like a Friday, the restaurant packed, the kitchen in high gear, the team working best when they were innovating.

Feb had been so engrossed in the kitchen that she hadn't made her usual guest rounds, which was how she'd almost missed two of her favorite people dining with them tonight. If she hadn't been standing next to Lacey when the dessert order came down the line—mango white chocolate panna cotta, no mint—she would have missed her friends completely.

"Amanda, so good to see you." She set the dessert plates on the table, the yuzu custard cupcake for Amanda, the panna cotta sans mint for her husband. "And Justin, you're glowing." She leaned in to hug them both, then slid into the chair across from Justin. "Everything good with the twins?"

He patted his extended belly, the baby bump prominent under his lavender suit and tie. Last time Feb had seen the married chefs at their restaurant, Diamond, Justin had just started showing. "Rooter and Tooter are great," he said, unleashing the Texas drawl he usually reined in.

Amanda rolled her eyes and stole a bite of his dessert. "We are not naming our children Rooter and Tooter."

He popped the back of her hand with his spoon. "Keep stealing my sweets, and we'll see about that."

Their laughter only subsided when Dylan appeared at their table with a tray of drinks, a flute of sparkling plum wine for Amanda, decaf coffee for Justin, and a whiskey for Feb. "You need anything else?" they asked.

"You two good?" Feb asked their guests. At her friends' nods, she smiled again at Dylan, coveting tonight's wine-red lipstick and matching gauge earrings. "We're good, thanks."

Justin's gaze tracked Dylan all the way back to the bar before he swung his dark, knowing stare Feb's direction. "So," he drawled. "Valentine's Day have anything to do with the cute bartender?"

As she considered how much to confess, Feb sipped her new favorite rye, one Dylan had introduced her to a couple weeks back. They'd been stocking the smooth Sonoma Coast whiskey ever since, and each night when Feb started her evening rounds, Dylan would bring her a glass. "I am interested," Feb admitted. "But they aren't the reason I'm opening for Valentine's Day. That's me giving two middle fingers to the critics."

Justin cackled. "That tracks."

"I loved what you did with the solo reservations," Amanda said.

"Should make it easy for that Render critic to go unnoticed, assuming he's still in town."

Feb bobbled her glass, nearly spilling her whiskey. "What Render critic?"

"Pretty sure we had one at Diamond last night," Justin said. "Reso was under Jacob Pappas?" he asked Amanda.

She nodded. "Average height, not an average body." She hummed her appreciation, and Justin tipped his mug in agreement. "Beefy, dark curls and darker eyes. Way too good-looking to be there alone."

"We tried to take him home and the blush on that bronze skin . . . Mmm!" He shimmied in his seat. "Almost as good as this panna cotta."

"I've seen a lot of food critics in my life, but never one that hot."

Feb chuckled at her friends' amusing back-and-forth, the two of them always on the hunt, but inside, her stomach was on a roller coaster. Justin must have noticed, his hand lightly covering hers on the table. "Hon, you okay?"

She shook her head. "Not really. I need to go see if Pappas is on the reservations list." Standing, she kissed both their cheeks before tossing back the rest of her whiskey and hauling ass across the dining room to the bar.

Dylan saw her coming, their eyes wide with concern. "What's wrong?"

"Is there a Jacob Pappas on the list for Valentine's?"

They grabbed the backbar tablet out of its holder and, after a couple taps, glanced back up at Feb. "Nine o'clock. Last seating."

She closed her eyes and tipped back her head, cursing the ceiling and whoever was up there giving *her* two middle fingers. "Fuck!"

———

Feb surveyed the kitchen one last time before flicking off the lights and making her way up the short, inclined breezeway to the dining room. While staff usually exited the back through the locker room, she'd learned a long time ago that if she didn't do a back-to-front walk-through on her way out, she'd spend the night worried that the espresso machine in the breezeway station was still on, or that the beer taps behind the bar were dripping, or that the front door wasn't locked. That her pride and joy, one way or another, would be destroyed by morning. She needed to lay eyes and hands on all the potential hazards on her way out or else she'd toss and turn all night and risk burning the place down herself the next day from exhaustion.

Espresso machine confirmed off, she continued on to the dining room—and stumbled to a stop at finding one of the barstools still occupied. Dylan sat angled toward the kitchen, their sticker-covered personal tablet propped up with a keyboard stand, Feb's favorite bottle of rye and two glasses waiting beside it.

"You're still here?" Feb said as she wove through the tables.

Dylan eyed her over the screen. "So are you."

Feb tossed her coat and bag out of the way on another stool, then climbed onto the one beside Dylan. She flicked her gaze at their tablet. "What are you doing?"

"Researching Jacob Pappas, which is definitely an alias."

Alias, not *fake name*. She'd noticed that about Dylan before; the precise way they spoke at certain times, usually about process or procedure, especially if it involved legal matters. Feb wondered if someone in their family was an attorney or in law enforcement. But that seemed too personal a question to ask without buildup, so she started with the safer, more immediate topic at hand. "That's the way Render critics work," she explained as she filled their glasses. "They can't let anyone know who they are or what they do. I only happen to know Pappas may be one because of Amanda and Justin."

Dylan closed the tablet and pushed it aside. "You seem calmer now."

"We stick with the plan. It's a good one." She was still nervous—she'd been waiting for a Render review for years —but she was more confident than ever in her team and her concept. "I'd be a helluva lot more fucked if we'd planned the boring prix fixe."

"Truth," Dylan said with a raised glass.

Feb clinked hers against it, then took a healthy swallow of the smooth, coastal rye. She leaned back against the padded barstool, eyeing Dylan's tablet again. "Who's the sticker fiend?"

Dylan's grin brimmed over with affection. "My niece," they said as they traced the giant clover at the center. "Her other aunt started her on stickers last St. Patrick's Day. It's been hell or hilarious ever since—jury's still out. Her dads' devices are completely covered."

"They're here in the city? Your family?"

They circled their hand in the air. "Around the Bay Area."

A local, then. As a transplant, Feb was always looking for a local's favorites. Locals knew where the good shit was buried—down this or that alley, tucked in beside one or the other storefront. They had their own map, separate and apart from the one critics and media pushed. "What's your favorite place to eat here?"

They shimmied in their seat. "We're sitting in it."

"Flatterer." Feb hid her pleased smile behind the rim of her glass, taking another sip before asking, "What's number two, then?"

"Angelica's Bakery."

Whiskey sloshed over the rim of Feb's glass as she banged it on the bar. "That place is *insane*. The mistletoe cannoli . . ." She mimed a chef's kiss, and even that wasn't praise enough for the best dessert—the best bakery—in town. She was only sad the too-short window for mistletoe cannoli had passed.

"They work well as bribes," Dylan said with a wink.

"You've tried that?"

"More like I was the bribed. Totally worth it."

Feb refilled their glasses. "It's good you have family around."

"I didn't always." Feb cocked a brow before she could stop herself from being nosy, but Dylan waved off her unspoken apology with an intentional flitter of their fingers, each nail painted a different color of the nonbinary pride flag. "My bio-fam kicked me out when I was a teen."

"Dyl—"

They shook their head and, improbably, smiled, as wide and affectionate as before when they'd spoken about their niece. "Best thing that ever happened to me. Sucked that first year I bounced around homeless, but I ended up in a queer teen shelter, and that was where I found my real family. I wouldn't have the family I chose without the ones who didn't choose me."

Feb swirled the rye in her glass, mimicking the guilt that swirled in her gut. "Now I feel like an ass for daily cursing mine for my name."

Dylan leaned in, their breath whispering across the side of Feb's face, their voice teasing and close. "They kind of deserve that one."

Feb laughed, the tense moment broken by the quick, dry wit she'd come to depend on the past few months. Feb thanked them by sharing the highlights of growing up February Winters. More laughter carried her and Dylan through another round of drinks, Feb starting to feel it, suspecting she'd feel it even more tomorrow morning, but she was too intrigued by Dylan to let this moment go. She wanted to get to know them better, had wanted to since they'd first walked through UTT's doors, but Feb was shit at making time outside the kitchen, especially for dates. Hell, even for friendships. But here, now, was the perfect opportunity to get to know one of the most intriguing people she'd met in . . . she couldn't remember how long.

And Dylan seemed intrigued by her too, more than happy to continue to get to know her better. "They treat you well, though, your family?" they asked.

"Incredibly," Feb answered with her own smile. "I'm lucky. They didn't blink when I said I wanted to cook for a living, didn't balk when I left Beaverton to move down here, and never once judged me for who I love." Her parents had only ever cheered her on, the loudest of her fans.

"Even if those relationships ended as broken hollandaise?"

She flopped back in her stool with a dramatic sigh. "They were *so* disappointed it didn't work out with Marissa. Mom thought she was the one." Marissa was a med student at UCSF, sweet, well-mannered, a dynamo in bed. Crazy busy, same as Feb. Neither of them took offense at the other's lack of time, but with virtually zero time together, their chemistry in the bedroom had zero time to bake into more. "As for Dad, he lobbied hard for Brett D'Moine at first."

Dylan slapped a hand over their mouth, barely keeping their whiskey in. Once they managed to swallow, they barked out a laugh. "Like the cheese? You can't be serious?"

"Oh, but I am," Feb sputtered around a giggle. "The irony was not lost on anyone. Too bad he wasn't nearly as tasty."

"You said *at first* about your dad, so when did it get stinky?"

"Well played," Feb said with a tip of her glass at the play on words. "Brett became my right hand in the kitchen where we both worked. I told him about the restaurant I wanted to open next. Then he stole the concept for his own place."

Dylan's outraged expression was the validation every chef who'd ever been in Feb's position—and there were plenty—craved. "He *didn't.*"

"Yep." She polished off the rest of her drink. "At least he had the good grace to take it to SoCal. The coyote wasteland can have him."

"So you swore off love for good?" Dylan said, as they poured Feb another.

"I didn't swear off love," she said with a flick of her hand. "I just didn't have time to go looking for it. Making real hollandaise every day is hard enough." She sipped at the whiskey and resteadied herself on her stool. "And if I wasn't going to trust anyone from the kitchen again, finding time out of it became impossible once I opened this place and it started to get attention."

"And your heart didn't."

"Heart, pfft." She leaned close to Dylan and affected the same conspiratorial whisper they'd used earlier. "I'd just settle for something besides my vibrator between my legs."

Feb giggled—until she noticed Dylan wasn't laughing. Those green eyes were fixed on her, their intense gaze fiery again, sending a zing right to where Feb used that vibrator. She giggled again, then pressed the back of her hand to her lips, trying to stop the words from tumbling out. "Did I just say that?"

Dylan's green gaze darkened. "You did."

"Too much whiskey." And if she didn't get off this stool right now, she was going to lean the rest of the way forward and break her own rule about smooching colleagues from the kitchen. She spun the opposite direction and vaulted off the stool. Teetering, she stayed upright solely by the grace of Dylan's hands around her biceps, their warm, compact body pressed against her back, their hot breath floating into the valley behind Feb's ear.

"Let me call you a car."

Feb's shiver creeped into her words. "I can walk."

She was sure Dylan noticed, the bartender skating their hands down Feb's arms, goose bumps lifting in their wake. "We can't let anything happen to you before the Render critic gets here." They lifted her arms from behind and braced them on the back of the adjacent stool. "You stay here. I'll finish locking up and get the rest of the lights." They made the lap around the dining room Feb hadn't finished earlier, flicking off lights as they went, casting more and more of the space in shadow. They cut through it with a grace and efficiency of movement Feb only seemed to have in the kitchen. Outside of it, she was the same nerdy kid who'd tripped up the bleachers during her third-grade choir recital.

Dylan ducked beneath the bar flip and strolled the length of the bar, checking all the taps were off and the top-shelf whiskey case secure.

The bar.

Dylan wasn't *really* in the kitchen. It wouldn't *really* be breaking any of Feb's rules to taste those wine-red lips and feel Dylan's body more firmly pressed against hers.

"Car should be here shortly," Dylan said as they

emerged from behind the other end of the bar, near where Feb waited. And waited, holding her tongue, letting the silence draw Dylan closer. "Feb, you okay?"

"There's another reason I haven't gone looking for a relationship lately." She shifted her weight from the stool to the person in front of her, looping her arms over their shoulders and resting her cheek against theirs, whispering her confession in Dylan's ear. "I haven't wanted to since you walked through my door."

TWO

Feb's lips were right there for the taking. A little chapped, slightly parted, terribly tempting. But acting on that temptation would be wrong. Not while Feb was drunk and not while she had no idea who she was really kissing.

Not Dylan Jacks, the edgy yet welcoming bartender who made sure everyone's glass at Under the Table was filled. That person was a very convincing character thanks to Helena Madigan's closet and the tireless coaching of undercover professionals.

No, the person in front of Feb, the one acting under Dylan Jacks's name and wearing Helena's leather, was Jax Dillon, the hacker who'd left behind a promising career in cyber law enforcement so they could chase bounties and contract targets with their family. More of the former these days, but still worlds away from Dylan Jacks.

Two very different people, both of whom wanted to kiss February Winters desperately. Jax's mouth was dry, their heart racing, their fingers itching to trail a path up Feb's back and into the long brown waves that were falling out of her topknot. This close, this tempted, they were struggling to hold on to their last thread of good intentions.

Until a familiar car horn blared, a life preserver tossed to a drowning person. Thank fuck.

Feb blew a raspberry as if the driver of the car could hear her. All it served to do was tickle Jax's neck and make them want to pull Feb closer, to feel her lips pressed firmly against their skin, to drown in the heat of her long, lean body, all her gangly, inked limbs atypically loose tonight. What would February Winters—unleashed of the tension and worry she usually carried—moan like, writhe like, taste like? Fuck if they were in a place to find out right now.

With a frustrated groan, Jax gently righted Feb, creating some much-needed space between them. "When you're not drunk, we'll talk about a better solution than your vibrator."

Feb's lopsided grin was both ridiculous and sexy. "I can talk now," she slurred.

"Yeah, no, chef. 'Fraid not." The car horn blared again. "And someone doesn't like to be kept waiting." Feb blew another raspberry but didn't resist as Jax coaxed her into her jacket, looped her crossbody bag over her shoulder, and snaked an arm around her waist. "Let's go," they said, starting them for the door. Outside, a chilly-for-San-Francisco wind whipped around them, causing Feb to shiver and lean closer, nuzzling her face into the crook of Jax's neck. The five steps to the curb where Helena's black SUV was idling were absolute torture.

Helena's knowing grin from behind the wheel didn't make it any better. "Your place or hers?"

"Hers." Jax rattled off the address as they settled Feb into the back seat. She was asleep, snoring softly, by the time Jax clicked the seat belt into place. They backed out, gently closed the door, then leaned through the open passenger window. "She may need some help getting in."

As if on cue, a honking snore carried from the back seat. "No shit," Helena said, eyes rolling, though the smile in her voice belied her amusement. "How that noise can come out of someone that pretty . . ." She shook her head, and Jax chuckled.

"I won't tell your wife you said that."

"Oh, Celia would agree." Helena winked, and Jax shook their head. Helena rarely minced words; she didn't have time as an attorney and as the head of the assassin side of the family. She was also an unrepentant flirt and one hundred percent devoted to her wife and family. "Special delivery for you. In the trunk."

"Mel confirmed?"

Helena nodded, and Jax bit back a wince. Jacob Pappas was indeed an alias—and a bigger problem than Feb realized. A Render review was the least of her worries.

"You need any help wiring?" Helena asked.

"Nope, I got it." They tapped the window ledge, then circled behind the car and retrieved the hard case from the trunk. Shutting the hatch, they waved at Helena in the rearview mirror. "Thank you."

"Owe me," Helena called back. She gunned the engine, and the Benz sped off, tires screeching. Jax smiled wider. Helena's vehicle of choice was a Ducati, but mom and auntie duties required something more practical. For the concession, Celia, one of the best mechanics in the city, had seriously jacked the already jacked AMG engine in the SUV. Jax wondered sometimes if Helena was having more fun in the Benz than on her bike these days.

Back inside, Jax checked their tablet and read the encrypted text from their boss. **Confirmed, wire it.**

On it, they texted Mel back.

HQ, 0200.

Jax glanced at the time: 1230. Ninety minutes. Tight, but doable.

———

Barely, it turned out.

It was exactly 0200 when Jax punched in their code to open the door to the South Beach condo that was home to Redemption Inc., the "consulting company" Jax had officially joined last year. The flickering light of the TV and the scent of fresh-brewed coffee lured them down the long entry hall to the main office area that had once been an open floor plan living space. Papers and caramel candy wrappers littered the conference table where a dining table used to be, the two workstations near the seismic struts and wall of balcony windows were empty, and stretched out on the leather couch in front of the TV was a long-limbed Daniel Talley, asleep in a wrinkled suit. Behind him, his wife and Jax's boss, Melissa Cruz, similarly dressed like she'd come from a night out, sat in Jax's usual spot in front of the wall of computers, nursing a cup of coffee and flipping through surveillance footage of UTT.

"All good?" Jax asked as they skirted behind Mel, on their way to the pantry that had been converted into a walk-in weapons and equipment safe.

"Reading well," Mel replied.

They spun the combo lock on the safe while warring voices squared off in their head. The guilty-sounding one cautioned that they were violating Feb's trust, from putting up cameras and mics to pretending to be someone they weren't. The other one argued they were protecting Feb; they were doing their job. They were neutralizing a threat before real injury came to Feb, UTT, and the staff Jax had come to consider friends. Jax needed to listen to the second voice. Didn't make their insides feel any less twisted up over the first.

"Everything okay?" Mel asked.

"Yeah, just need caffeine," Jax covered as they finished putting away the leftover surveillance equipment. They closed and secured the safe behind them, swung through the kitchen for a cup of joe, then claimed the desk chair next to Mel. "He's the bounty, right?" They jutted their chin at the photo of Jacob Pappas onscreen. "Trent Mendes. Former CIA."

Mendes had been tossed out of the agency and charged with mishandling classified information. As his trial neared and rumors swirled that he'd sold said information to third parties, he'd pulled a Casper and disappeared. Mostly. Redemption had tracked him to California, then, using credit card history from before he'd disappeared, they'd determined Mendes was a foodie who couldn't resist the hottest spots. Accordingly, they'd placed operatives in restaurants up and down the state. Now, they had a good lead on which one he'd be dining at next—Under the Table.

"Once I had a name to go on," Jax said, "I was able to pull more footage."

"It's him." With a few clicks of the mouse, Mel opened Mendes's CIA headshot next to the photo still Jax had nabbed off a traffic cam at the intersection outside Diamond. His hair was darker now, his eye color altered, and his nose sported a new bump, but Jacob Pappas was Trent Mendes according to the facial recognition software. According to Jax's eyes too; seeing them side by side, they could spot the resemblance. "I've got the rest of the team pulling his Render reviews," Mel said. "We'll piece together more of the timeline. Where he's been, his connections, where he might be hiding out. It was a clever cover."

"What do you need me to do?" Jax asked. "Should I retire Dylan?"

"Why would you do that?" Mel minimized the windows onscreen and, coffee in hand, rotated her chair and assessing brown gaze in Jax's direction. "You're on the scene, and I got the impression you liked bartending."

"I do. Paid part of my way through college." The Madigans—their chosen family—had paid the rest. "It's good being back behind the bar."

"So, what's the problem?"

They could continue weaving and dodging, but that would be futile. Mel was a former FBI Special Agent in Charge and the best interrogator Jax knew. Yes, Jax had picked up more than just ace hacker skills from their family, including the basics of detective and undercover work, but even their best ruse wouldn't stand the test of Mel's skills. And if—once—Mel saw Jax and Feb on the surveillance feed together, there'd be no denying the truth, assuming Helena didn't tattle on her first. "I like her," Jax admitted.

Mel cocked a perfectly plucked brow. "Which her? You gotta be a bit more specific."

Jax laughed and relaxed back in their chair. "February, the head chef. She's talented, she's tough but civil in the kitchen, and she's one of us. She's queer." The Madigans and their associates, Mel included, were active in the

LGBTQIA+ community and had built their own queer found family over the years. Hell, found family was what held Redemption Inc. together. Feb had built a similar family at UTT and with other queer chefs in the city, like Amanda and Justin. Jax admired her for the community she'd fostered and for her voice as a chef, for the concept —a second one—she'd formulated and run with. She deserved recognition for all she'd done, and that recognition would go further than UTT's walls. "A Render review, even if the dude is a wanted traitor, would cement Feb and Under the Table on all the best of lists and lift others too."

"She's not already on those lists? A simple internet search returns dozens of articles, all of them saying she'll get her stars and a Beard soon."

"She is and she will . . ." The minute the open-ended sentence was out, Jax face-palmed. The unintentional ellipses were the kind of open door Mel would walk right through.

And she did, a grin tickling one corner of her mouth. "You like her more than just professionally." Not a question, an observation that was one hundred percent accurate.

Jax averted their gaze and sipped their coffee. The longer this conversation went on, the more they swung toward staying undercover at UTT. But the longer it went on, the more ammunition she gave Mel to take them off the op.

Mel tapped a toe against their shin and waited for their attention. "This life, Jax, what we do, what our families do, on both sides of the law, is not easy for civilians to understand." Her smirk softened into a gentler smile, one tempered by experience and caution. It came through in her voice too. "Truth, it's downright hard to survive sometimes."

Jax hung their head. "Ugh, Mel, not helping."

Chuckling, she gave their shin another couple of taps, this time in commiseration. "Helena makes it work. I make it work, and my husband is the definition of civilian who steps into shit."

"I heard that, chica," Danny rumbled from the other side of the couch.

They both laughed, which warmed Jax's insides better than any coffee. Mel's hand on their knee, squeezing gently, was another shot of friendly, encouraging warmth. "It's not easy," she said. "But it's not impossible."

THREE

When Jax entered the UTT kitchen later that day, they barely missed colliding with Juan, who, with a curse, pitched a smoking saucepan onto the teetering tower of dirties in the dishwasher's industrial double sink. Their dishwasher, Adam, cursed in reply, sweat dripping from beneath the bandana over his brow. Neither seemed to notice Jax, who stepped out of the way just in time to avoid a second collision with Juan as he trudged back to his station. Shoulders slumped, he grabbed another saucepan to apparently try again, the heavy-bottom pot clanging as it came down hard on the burner grate.

Wide-eyed, Jax glanced around the kitchen and quickly concluded Juan wasn't the only chef on edge. Lots of creased brows, short words, and messy stations. The entire kitchen was off, which Jax had expected to some degree today—they were test driving the Valentine's Day menu tonight—but not this level of chaotic misery. This was not the kind of kitchen Feb ran.

Or maybe not Feb? Jax swept their gaze around the

space once more. No sign of Feb and her messy topknot anywhere.

Concern spiking, Jax carefully but swiftly crossed to Adi's station where the sous-chef was using tweezers to peel back the delicate, wrinkly skin of a morel mushroom. "Where's Feb?" they asked, trying to keep the worry out of their voice, sensing it was the last thing Adi needed right then.

"In the dining room," Adi replied with an uncharacteristic growl.

"Has she been back here lately?"

Adi snagged a tiny measuring spoon and gently scooped out the crab stuffing inside the mushroom. "Not once."

Jax checked the time on their tablet. "It's ninety minutes to service. Did anyone try to talk to her?"

Adi finished her delicate task and straightened with a huff. She closed her eyes and hung back her head, taking a long deep breath before righting her gaze and snatching a piece of paper off the adjacent expeditor's station. She handed the sheet to Jax. "It didn't go well."

Jax skimmed the menu they knew by heart, except this copy of tonight's line-up was covered with strikethroughs and scribbles in Feb's familiar chicken scratch. "What is this?"

"A list of revisions to the menu. And she said more would be coming."

Suddenly, the collective stress made sense. Feb would occasionally tweak dishes on the fly—a splash more sauce, leave the head on the fish, use edible flowers instead of chopped herbs for plating—but Feb's revisions to the V-day menu weren't minor tweaks. This was an overhaul of practically every dish. Too many changes all at once for a special dinner no one expected to be cooking in the first place. It was asking too much, even of these chefs, and totally not the kind of chef and boss Feb was.

"I'll talk to her," Jax said. "In the meantime, tell everyone to stop and clean." It wasn't their place in the kitchen hierarchy to give the order, but the chefs would listen to their sous, especially in Feb's absence. But would the sous listen to them? Adi had every right to tell Jax to go jump in a lake too, and her cocked hip made Jax think she might do just that. Jax hoped not. They liked these people and wanted to help settle the chaos so UTT could shine tonight, like Jax knew they would. With the original menu. Not to mention, they were injecting enough chaos already, even if no one knew it. "Let me try," Jax pleaded. "And let everyone else have a breather before someone breaks someth—"

A glass shattered behind them.

"Else," Adi said, lips twitching. "Something *else*. I've lost count of the shatters today." She rolled her eyes before her gaze settled back on Jax. "Give it a go. None of the rest of us could talk sense into her."

They nodded, waited for Lacey to pass in a chocolate-stained haze, then hustled for the breezeway. As they passed Feb's empty chef's nook, Jax mentally cursed themselves for not checking the surveillance feeds earlier. They'd sent a text to HQ, confirmed all was good, then steadfastly ignored the temptation to check the feeds themselves, determined not to invade Feb's and UTT's privacy any more than they had to. Maybe if they had, they could have helped sooner.

Jax stepped into the dining room, also mentally cursing

their Redemption colleagues too. They should've alerted them, but in fairness, how would they have known what they were seeing was so out of the norm? They weren't the ones who'd worked at UTT the past three months; they wouldn't understand how strange the sight before them was. Two of the room's tables were covered with printouts—was that also a calendar and almanac on one?—and the bar was similarly strewn with paper, some scribbled-on sheets, some balled up, the mess interrupted every so often by a coffee mug.

And at the far end of the bar sat a bedraggled-looking Feb. Gone were her usual contacts, replaced by glasses that were halfway down her nose; more of her long, caramel-colored locks had escaped her topknot than were in it, and her chef's coat looked like it had been through the service from hell, stained with handprints and splashes of various colors. As Jax drew closer, they could also see the barely-there freckles on Feb's nose and cheeks that were usually only visible toward the end of service, her light dusting of makeup worn off for the night. How long had she been at this today?

Jax lifted the bar flip and skirted behind the bar, calling out a "Hey, Feb" when they were halfway to her, aiming not to startle.

Feb didn't bother to glance up, just flicked her pen in greeting before putting it back to paper, lining out some-thing else. "Can you make me a London Fog? Adi tried, and it wasn't the same. I think she used vanilla instead of honey."

Both were in a London Fog, not one instead of the other, and Feb knew that. She'd worked with Lacey last month on a deconstructed version of the tea latte for a dessert course.

Someone definitely wasn't thinking clearly. She'd probably also had enough caffeine for the rest of the week, judging by the number of dirty mugs on the bar. Jax poured her a glass of water instead and slid it in front of her. "Adi said you weren't cooking yet today. Your chef's coat says otherwise."

"At home," she answered.

"Since when?"

"Four."

But it was only four-thirty. She must have meant she'd been cooking at home before getting here at four. "So you just got here?"

"In the morning," she corrected. "Got here at noon."

Jax leaned forward, their forearms braced on the bar. "Feb, you left here at twelve-thirty in the morning." No response, just more scribbling. Jax nudged the glass of water closer. "Does your cooking marathon have anything to do with the menu revisions?"

Finally noticing the glass, Feb exchanged her pen for the water and took a giant gulp, giving Jax the distraction they needed to swipe the pen. Lowering the glass, Feb immediately looked again for it; when she couldn't find what she was looking for, she began checking under the stacks of paper. "Where'd my pen go?" She slid off the stool, looked beneath it too, then back up at Jax. "Did you see where my pen went?"

"Can you tell me what this"—Jax gestured at the chaos in their immediate vicinity—"is all about?"

Feb spun on her heel and shuffled papers on the nearest table. "I read all of Pappas's reviews. Made a list of things he's critical of or doesn't like. Here!" She twirled back around and slapped a piece of paper on the bar. One edge was singed, and the other was stained with something green. "We needed to make revisions."

Among the many words underlined, circled, and struck through, *MORELS* caught Jax's eye. "Is this why Adi is scooping the crab out of the mushrooms?"

Feb shoved a different printout at Jax. "This article."

They skimmed the review, becoming more confused with each passing sentence. "Feb, this says he wanted *more* morels."

"Exactly!" She flung her hands in the air, her arms like wet noodles as they flopped back to her side. "How am I supposed to know what's the right amount? We should just eighty-six them. Fuck!" She jammed a hand in her hair, the rest of the knot falling around her face, which she didn't seem to notice as she spun back to the table. "There was something else I just saw . . ."

Jax stepped out from behind the bar and over to the table. More lists, more of Pappas's reviews, more words underlined, circled, and struck through.

Chicken.

Peas.

Seafood.

The last was enough to make Jax's Bay Area soul shudder. "For fuck's sake, Feb, this is San Francisco. If there's not seafood something on the menu, it's a red flag. You gonna toss the sourdough too?"

"There was a remark here," she said, pushing one review pile off the table and digging into another. "But I didn't—"

Jax grasped her wrist and turned her away from the table. "Babe, you need to chill." Feb's blue eyes widened; whether from the *babe* or the fact someone broke through the haze, Jax didn't know. And didn't care. They had a teeny tiny opening; they had to take it. "We need to get out of here." They needed to get Feb someplace her mind could get off Pappas and the V-day menu long enough for her good senses to return. Jax knew just the place, her conversation with Feb last night coming to mind.

But convincing Feb to detach herself from the panic was proving difficult. "We can't! We have service!"

She tried to wrest her arm free, but Jax had been trained in hand-to-hand combat by experts. There was no getting loose unless Jax allowed her. That said, they didn't want to cause Feb more panic, and by the rapid rise and fall of her chest, that was where this was headed. Too quickly. They eased their hold, a thumb sliding against the underside of Feb's wrist and over her hammering pulse. "You need to breathe, Feb. You need to take a break."

"But service—"

Another swipe of their thumb, and Feb stopped struggling. Her shoulders slumped, her chin dipped the same direction, and exhaustion appeared in the cracks of Feb's caffeine-fueled anxiety. Jax stepped closer, a gentle hand around her biceps, slowly rubbing up and down in time with their even breaths, waiting for Feb's to slow and match. "Tell Adi to go back to the original menu, then let her handle first seating. Mo can hold down the bar without me for a few." They squeezed Feb's arms. "Trust me."

Feb's trust lasted only as long as the short cab ride from Jackson Square to North Beach. As soon as they climbed out of the car, even as Jax rotated Feb to face their destination, she was trying to get back to UTT. "Dylan, I love baked goods as much as the next person, and Angelica's is the best in the city, but we don't have time for this."

Jax closed the distance between them, their front pressed to Feb's back, their hands lightly cupping her shoulders. Pitching their voice low, aiming to distract again, they spoke right next to Feb's ear. "What we don't have time for is you losing your shit."

A shiver rippled through Feb, and a shuddery breath later, Feb relaxed in their hold. "I don't want to fuck this up. We might never get another shot at a Render review."

"You won't fuck it up." Jax gave her arms a squeeze, then reluctantly stepped back and rounded to stand between her and the bakery's plate glass window. They waited for Feb to lift her chin, wanting the chef to see the confidence in their gaze. "You'll get your stars."

"You can't be sure."

"I am, because I've tasted your food and worked with you for the past three months. You're *that good* and everyone who works with you wants it too. They want it *for you*."

Feb's answering blush was a welcome respite, her anxiety receding enough for compliments to sink in. Now to push her worry the rest of the way back. Jax jutted a thumb over their shoulder. "Everything inside AB's is good too. How about we go reset the day?"

Inside, they'd just hung their coats on the wall pegs when a shout of "Jax!" rang out from behind the counter. Panic spiked, then eased as Jax mentally thanked their mentors for all those undercover tips about using a cover name close to their own. Feb hadn't seemed to notice Mia calling Jax by what Feb thought was their last name. Helena's stepdaughter hustled out from behind the counter, her long dark hair gathered into a braid over one shoulder, her apron and cheeks dusted with flour. "I have that favor ready for you."

"Excellent," Jax said as they gave her a sideways hug. "Thanks for pulling it together so fast."

"Just don't tell my uncle. I cut off his friends and family benefits at the end of January."

Jax laughed, then, with a hand to Feb's back, drew her closer. "Mia, I'd like you to meet February Winters, one of the best chefs in the city. Feb, this is Mia Perri—you're gonna want to keep an eye on her. She's one hell of a baker."

Mia circled a hand in the air before holding it out for Feb to shake. "Like I could escape that fate."

"You love it," Jax said.

"I really do," she conceded with the same wide, easy smile as her mother.

"Wait, Perri?" Feb said as she withdrew her hand. "As in Angelica Perri? You're part of the family who owns this place?"

"I am," Mia said with a nod. "Angelica is my mom's cousin." At nineteen, Mia was already second in command at AB's, running the bakery with Angelica while also getting her degree at Golden Gate University. "And Jax—"

"Would love two London Fogs," they said, cutting Mia off before their cover was well and truly blown. In retrospect, they probably should have given Mia more of a heads-up than just their own friends and family request, but like all the Perris, Mia caught on fast and knew when not to ask questions.

"Comin' right up, along with that other order," she added with a wink. "Grab a table, and I'll bring them out."

Jax steered a seemingly dazed Feb toward an out-of-the-way booth in the far corner. Once they were seated, Jax waved a hand in front of her face and teased, "You still in there?"

Feb blinked. "Yeah, sorry." She gave a sharp shake of her head, as if she were clearing away the lingering surprise. "I knew you were a local from when we talked before, but I didn't expect to walk in here and have the staff know you by name. Was Mia the one who bribed you with the mistletoe cannoli?"

"Her uncle."

"It's all starting to come together."

Before Feb could catch on to Jax's surprise, they swerved a different direction, asking, "So, why the freak-out? I know what you said outside"—they flitted their fingers toward the window—"but *you* know you're damn good and you usually don't give a fuck what others think, especially the critics."

She gathered her hair into a fresh knot, more of the Feb that Jax knew coming back online. "I want everyone to think that because that's the vibe I want for UTT. We do things our way, period. But I'm a perfectionist like any other chef at this level, and I want everyone's sacrifices to be worth it." She propped her elbows on the table and scrubbed her hands over her face, fingers sneaking under her glasses to rub her eyes. "And if I fail, on Valentine's Day of all days, it'll be like every other . . ." She lowered her arms, folded them on the table, and buried her head in them. "Ugh, I don't want to be this person still."

Her words were muffled but loud enough for Jax to

hear. Chuckling, they gently tugged an arm free so they could see the side of Feb's face. "Every other what?"

Feb angled her chin, giving Jax a better view of her miserable expression. "I never got a rose."

"For?"

She laid her head on her folded arms, and the sadness that floated over her delicate features caused a pinch in Jax's chest. "Valentine's Day," she said. "In middle and high school, student groups would sell roses and deliver them in class. I never got one."

Ah. Jax remembered that practice and regarded it as hurtful and obnoxious as Feb did. For them, Valentine's Day had also brought more nagging from their parents to put on makeup and dress more like a girl so they could land a boy, neither of which interested Jax. Granted, they'd grown up to wear dresses on occasion, even makeup some-times, but on their own terms. Jax was fairly certain their parents would've never approved of the sparkling mini they'd worn to the annual Madigan-Talley New Year's party or the smoky eye they regularly wore for their bar shifts at UTT.

The bar.

Jax had the perfect antidote to both their woes. A drink they'd learned from a certain cowboy hacker from Texas who, like Jax, was part of the extended Madigan clan.

"I know what my drink is going to be for Valentine's Day."

Feb lifted her torso and sat back against the booth, interest sparking again in her blue eyes. "What's that?"

"A Blue Rose."

"Don't make it blue because I told you a pity-me story."

With their hand near Feb's on the table, Jax tangled their

fingers like they'd wanted to for months, the fit better and more natural than they could've imagined. "It's blue because of your eyes. And because you're making it a special night for everyone there. I can make sure they each get a rose too."

"Dylan," Feb gasped softly, her fingers tightening with purpose around Jax's. Then tugging, using Jax's hand in hers to pull them half across the table, surprising Jax with chapped lips skating lightly over theirs, the tip of her tongue flicking the seam of their lips, seeking entrance.

Someone cleared her throat beside the table. "I'm guessing you don't need these now," Mia said. "I'll just keep them."

Jax was torn—part their lips and deepen the kiss with Feb or claim the gift Mia had for Feb? The latter won, barely. They drew back, smiling, first for Feb, then for Mia, as they snatched the pastry box from her hands as politely as possible. "Oh no, those are mine."

"Good thing I know the recipe." Mia's eyes flickered down to their joined hands, then, with a knowing smirk that reminded Jax all too much of her stepmom, turned on her heel back toward the kitchen.

Jax laughed, louder still at Feb's dramatic "What's in the box?"

They pushed it across the table. "For you."

She peeked under the lid and her eyes grew round as saucers, her smile stretching across her face. "Mistletoe cannoli? How?"

They shrugged. "Doesn't matter how. Just that it made you smile."

Feb's fingers clenched around theirs again. "Will you go

out with me on Tuesday after we survive the Valentine's Day service?"

Jax thought that ask, the Valentine's Day it promised, better than any rose they'd never received. "I'd love to."

————

Jax counted the break at AB's a success. Feb had left with a belly full of cannoli and her mind firing again on all cylinders, scaling back her V-day menu revisions to only a few necessary changes. Jax had left with a kiss they would have liked to enjoy again after service, but by the time they'd finished closing down the bar, Feb had already left. Adi had spied her swaying against the expeditor's station, eyelids and shoulders drooping. She'd sent her home as soon as the last soufflé had left the kitchen. As much as Jax would've loved that after-work kiss, they wouldn't have been able to enjoy it for long anyway. A text from Braxton Kane, Jax's former boss at SFPD and Mel's partner at Redemption Inc., had summoned them to HQ.

When they arrived, they were surprised by the person sitting with Brax at the conference table.

"Jax," Isaiah Fletcher said as he stood and offered his hand. "It's good to see you." The Internal Affairs detective gave them a small smile, his usual reserved self, but Jax could read the sincerity in his bloodshot brown eyes. Some considered Fletcher cold, but he'd always been kind and patient with them, and when it had come to Brax's kidnapping a few years back, Fletcher had done everything in his power to help bring him home. He was a good man, if a bit of a loner. "We miss you at the station."

Jax missed the station too, but they would have missed

working with Brax and his husband, Holt Madigan, more. Holt, one of Helena's brothers, had been the first person to connect with Jax at the Madigans' queer teen shelter. Holt had recognized their skill with a computer, had put them on the path to a computer science degree, then had mentored them in the art of hacking, something he'd excelled at in the military before joining the family business as a digital assassin.

There'd ultimately been no way to avoid the conflicts of interest between the department and the Madigans' illegal activities. Brax, as well as Mia's uncle—a former ATF agent who was married to Hawes, Helena's other brother—had made the same decision. Redemption Inc. allowed Jax and Brax to settle somewhere in the middle professionally, and their organization had delivered more than a few bounties to SFPD.

"I can find excuses to come around more often," they said to Fletcher. "Working a line on a bounty right now."

Fletcher winced as he sank back into his chair, raking a hand through his disheveled blond hair. In fact, all of him looked uncharacteristically disheveled, from his missing tie to his wrinkled, rolled-up shirtsleeves to the mismatched socks shoved into his loafers. Granted, it was past midnight on a Friday—Saturday, technically—but Jax recalled weekend all-nighters at the station when Fletcher hadn't looked half as roughed up as he did now.

They lowered themself into the chair on Fletcher's other side. "What's going on?"

"We need to talk about Jacob Pappas," Brax said.

"Trent Mendes," Jax corrected.

"That's who you think he is?" Fletcher asked.

Nodding, Jax pulled their tablet from their bag and

opened it on the table, bringing up the surveillance footage they'd reviewed with Mel. Two photos in, Fletcher spun and shot out of his chair. Something was definitely up. "I repeat," Jax said, "what's going on?"

Head bowed, Fletcher clasped his hands behind his neck. "It's him."

"Are you—" Brax began, only to be cut off by Fletcher's sharp retort.

"Yes, I'm sure." He turned and the pinch of sadness Jax had earlier felt for Feb was nothing compared to the gut punch they felt at the expression clouding Fletcher's features. One Jax recognized all too well. The look—the feeling—of being left behind, of being unwanted. "I think I'd know my own husband."

Jax nearly fell out of their chair. "What?" They were expecting an ex-lover, maybe. Or family. But husband? "We dug into you when Brax was blackmailed. There's no record of you being married."

"It was annulled." He crossed back to the chair and lowered into it. "And you and Holt aren't the only top-shelf hackers out there." He pulled the tablet closer, staring longingly at the man onscreen. "Trent Mendes isn't even his real name. That's why he never crossed my radar. But Pappas . . ." He rotated away from the tablet. "It was his mother's maiden name."

"And your middle name?" Brax prompted.

"Jacob," Jax answered before Fletcher could, remembering that bit of information from their prior research. "Did he want to be found?"

"That's what I'm starting to wonder," Fletcher said, slumping in his chair with his eyes closed. "He always was a foodie."

"What's his real name, Fletcher?" Brax said.

"To me, he was Leo Flores." He propped his elbows on the table and dragged his hands over his face. "In truth . . ." He dropped his arms and split a glance between them. "He's Ariel Camino."

Jax's gasp collided with Brax's beleaguered groan. "The missing heir to the Camino Cartel?" he said.

"That's the one," Fletcher replied, expression grim.

As was Jax's assessment of this case, which had just gotten exponentially more dangerous, especially for the woman they were falling for.

FOUR

"We're the lead in Eater's not-to-miss Valentine's post."

Spinning toward Lacey's excited voice, Feb nearly spilled the salmoriglio sauce she'd been perfecting with Juan. "You're joking."

Bricks of butter in one arm, Lacey lifted her phone with the other, screen facing out, the familiar red and white Eater banner visible. "Not a joke. One of their bloggers was here Friday."

"Fucking hell," Feb cursed. How had she missed them? She couldn't recall seeing any of the local Eater crew in the dining room or on the reservation list, and she'd been watching both like a hawk since the Render news. An out-of-town reviewer, maybe? Had they visited when she'd been at AB's with Dylan? She wouldn't trade those couple hours away for anything. She'd needed them—probably wouldn't have the glowing early reviews without them—and she certainly didn't regret the brush of lips and promise of more the impromptu break had netted. But what had she missed during her absence? What if everything had gone wrong instead of right? Had it gone right?

"Well, what's it say?" Adi asked, beating Feb to the question.

Lacey dumped the butter on the cold block at her station, then read from her phone, voice raised for the entire kitchen to hear. "While only an early glimpse of what Chef Winters has in store for her Valentine's Day diners, this foodie wishes they were among those on the list for the culinary wooing Under the Table promises Tuesday night. Our most exciting new entrant to the San Francisco V-day scene."

Adi cheered and pumped her fist. "Fuck yeah!"

Feb high-fived Juan's oven-mittened hand, then again when Chloe shouted out their mentions in Cyn Eats and SFGate.

"Ooh!" Lacey piped up again. "Coverage in InsideHook too. 'Chef Winters's V-day menu is a uniquely satisfying approach to the industry's second worst day of the year.'"

"They better not expect the same for Mother's Day." Despite her change of heart on V-day, Feb would forever refuse to do anything but her annual found family staff meal on the industry's absolute worst day. "Hard pass."

"Hear, hear!" rang out around the kitchen, as did laughter and cheers, everyone riding the high of the positive early reviews.

Maybe they could pull this off; V-day, the UTT way. The way a certain talented, sexy bartender had helped Feb see. If only Dylan was there to celebrate too. They'd called out yesterday—a text sent to Mo, asking him to cover their shift. And now it was less than an hour to Sunday's first seating and no sign of them.

Had Feb been too forward at AB's by pulling Dylan into that kiss? She didn't think so. Dylan had agreed to the date Tuesday night, but even rewinding further, they'd been flirtatious on the sidewalk outside AB's, whispering hotly in her ear and pressed all along her backside. Then inside, they'd been tactile the entire time, even in front of folks they knew. And they'd returned that kiss. Feb was ninety-nine percent sure it would have veered toward indecent if Mia hadn't shown up at their table. Was Dylan having second thoughts now? Or if the kiss wasn't the thing keeping Dylan away, then was it Feb leaving Friday night without saying goodbye?

She'd been dead on her feet that night. Adi had put her in a cab, and she'd slept the entire ride home. Once there, she'd fallen into bed, fully dressed, asleep without a second thought, including to call Dylan, which she did finally remember the next morning. But then she'd decided it would be better to apologize in person, except Dylan hadn't been at UTT yesterday for her to do so. Had she let things go too long now without saying something? Wouldn't be the first time she'd been waiting for the right time to do something, only for the right time to fly right by, usually to disastrous consequence. See Brett D'Moine and the restaurant that should have been. Feb did not want to miss her opportunity with Dylan; folks who got her on the level they did came around so seldom, even less so ones that also sparked such a fiery attraction. Something in her gut told Feb that Dylan was special, and as a chef, she'd learned to trust what her stomach told her. And the way it was dipping now . . . she was increasingly terrified she'd fucked things up. Were they still even on for their date night? Feb hoped so, but if Dylan didn't show today, and with tomorrow just being prep—

Adi appeared beside her, a hand on her shoulder. "Hey, you okay?"

"Yeah, sorry." She gave her head a shake. "Was just going over the menu again."

"We're not making more changes, are we?" Adi asked with a quirked brow. "I think all the positive coverage proves we're on the right track."

"She's right," said the voice Feb most wanted to hear. She jerked her chin up, her gaze locking with the confident green one across the room. Dylan stood at the entrance to the locker room, their grin full of pride. "You've got nothing to worry about."

Exhaling, Feb returned Dylan's smile, the first real one since Friday. Until smoke tickled her nose and Chloe's "Fuck!" drew her attention elsewhere.

The line cook yanked a tray of smoking, charred veg from the oven. "That's the butternut squash gone for tonight."

Dylan's smile morphed into a knowing smirk, and Feb hoped like hell she wasn't imagining the same heat that had bubbled between them Friday. She didn't think so, as Dylan's eyes heated just before they nodded for her to get to it. With the countdown clock to their date ticking again, Feb was more than happy to do just that, time passing faster when she was busy. Calmer, more focused, she turned her attention back to her chefs. "All right, let's work the problem. We need a different soup tonight."

"Sunchokes?" Chloe said, coming back strong. "Relatively simple soup. Should be ready in time for service."

"Let's do it."

———

Feb was in her chef's nook, scribbling after-service notes, when a drink appeared beside her notepad. The color was the same bright blue as the nails of the person who delivered it. *Miami* was the first thought that popped to mind, and a second thought later, Feb laughed out loud.

"What's so funny?" Dylan asked, a smile in their voice.

Feb closed her notebook, picked up the drink, and rotated on her stool toward where Dylan was leaning against the doorless nook's molding. They'd changed out of their service leather into their casual nerd attire, which clashed even further with the Miami Vice of it all, causing Feb to giggle again. "The color of this"—she lifted the glass—"made me think of Miami, and then I saw your nails were painted the same, and I thought of you in Miami." Dylan scrunched up their nose and pursed their lips, a sour expression that made Feb laugh harder. "I didn't think you'd be a fan."

"Correct," Dylan said. "Too much sun." They gestured with a hand in the air at their surroundings. "I come from the land of fog."

"And yet this"—Feb shimmied the glass, the little umbrella in it tipping from one side to the other—"appears distinctly tropical."

"Umbrella was to make you laugh."

"Succeeded."

Dylan's shy victory made Feb want to lean forward, grab them by their T-Rex printed tie, and haul them in for a kiss, but they started talking again before Feb could act on the simmering desire.

"As for the drink, it's actually Texan." At Feb's raised

brow, Dylan explained further. "Visited a friend of the family from down that way last year, and I had one of those while I was in town." They nodded toward the glass. "They call it a Blue Rose. I made a few tweaks. Classed it up a bit."

"I won't tell your Texan friend you said that. And the nails?"

They flitted them in the air. "Had another friend familiar with the drink paint them so I could get the color right." Feb raised her other brow. Dylan didn't seem the sort to forget details, especially given this was a drink they recalled from a visit, not one they poured regularly. "I'm color-blind," they explained. "Needed a reference to match. Blues are tricky for me."

And yet they were going out of their way to make a blue drink for the V-day menu, trying to right a past wrong done to Feb, and doing so within the confines of Feb's no-pink rule. All little facts that heated Feb up inside, that made the simmer between them kick up in intensity.

And kick up more as soon as Feb took a sip of the intriguing, surprising drink full of the contradictions she couldn't get enough of. She'd expected the blue curaçao giving the drink its color to be the dominant flavor, but the bitter, orangey flavor of the liquor was balanced perfectly by a one-two punch of smooth tequila with subtle heat and a smoky mezcal that absorbed the burn of its agave sibling, before a blast of freshness—lime and another flavor Feb couldn't quite place—subtly recentered the orange. "What's the secret ingredient? Besides the tequila-mezcal duo."

"Caught that, did you?"

She grinned. "Something that brings out the sweetness of the orange, not the bitter. Guava?"

"Close. Passionfruit."

"That's it!" She took another taste, savoring as she picked out each flavor, the journey of the drink in a single sip the kind of thing a chef—definitely a foodie—would geek out over. "This is wonderful, Dylan."

The rosy blush that colored their winter pale cheeks was lovely. Feb itched again to reach out and pick up where they'd left off at AB's, but Dylan filled the silence again first. "I also made a blueberry-rosemary-orange shrub," they said. "We can use it for soda water or champagne for those who don't want the hard liquor. They'll still get their rose."

"Thank you," Feb said, as much for herself as for her diners who Dylan had gone out of their way to make feel special. "You didn't have to do all this, but they'll appreciate it. *I* appreciate it."

Blush deepening, Dylan averted their gaze, tracking Feb's hand as she set the glass aside, then sliding to her open notebook still on the counter. "You still making menu revisions?"

"The sunchoke soup was a hit tonight. Swapping it out."

"You're always making it work."

Feb took a deep breath, then stepped into the opening Dylan had presented. "I was afraid I hadn't with you."

Dylan continued to look anywhere but at Feb. Not a good sign. Was the spark Feb felt between them one-sided? Was she just imaging the heat in their gaze and the invitation in their smile? Was Dylan just being polite and professional? Had Feb really fucked things up that badly? "I'm sorry that I just left Friday night."

They ducked their chin and ran a hand over the back of their neck. Feb sensed they would've run it over their head too if not for the mohawk. "It's not you," they said, then immediately jerked their chin up, apology swirling in their green gaze. "Fuck, scratch that. No one ever wants to hear that line." They dropped their hand, and for the first time that night, Feb glimpsed the tension they'd been hiding all service long. The tightness in their shoulders and back, the divot between their eyes, the clench and fist of their hands, like even their fingers hurt. "Some family shit hit the fan. That was where I was yesterday."

"Is everyone okay?"

Dylan swiped Feb's drink and drained the rest of it. "TBD."

"If you need to take more time—"

"I need to be here," Dylan said, stepping closer as if they couldn't help it, and hope flared inside Feb. She shifted on her stool, heels propped on the rung so her knees were bent on either side of Dylan's hips. "Feb," Dylan murmured, equal parts want and warning in their voice.

Feb took her chances on the first, snagging the end of their tie and drawing them closer. "Are we still on for Tuesday night?"

"I shouldn't," Dylan said, even as their expression said the opposite.

"Why?"

"Said family shit. I love them, but it's complicated."

"Let's try not complicated." Feb drew them the rest of the way in, straightening so they were at eye level, noses and lips a scant distance apart. "Do you want to go out with me Tuesday night?"

"Yes." Zero hesitation.

Feb grinned. "Do you want me to kiss you right now?"

"Fuck yes."

Green light.

And Feb didn't hesitate to speed ahead, slamming their mouths together and claiming the kiss she'd wanted all night. Had fantasized about the past two days. Hell, since Dylan Jacks had first entered her restaurant. Dylan didn't hold back either, their tongue tangling with Feb's, their arms circling her neck and resting on Feb's shoulders, their body as snug to Feb's as it could be given their position and clothing.

Shame, that. The nook, barely larger than an airplane bathroom, didn't hold nearly the possibilities of the bar, or better yet, a bed at her place or Dylan's. Some place she could kiss and tease every inch of the rockin' body her hands were skating over, could see if the rest of Dylan flushed as lovely as their cheeks, could find out if the graceful movements she vaguely remembered through the whiskey haze of the other night held true as Dylan came apart at the seams from pleasure.

Dylan rocked their hips, causing Feb to moan, to drop a hand lower and clutch an ass cheek, holding Dylan closer, craving the friction. "Fuck, Feb," Dylan gasped against her lips. "Tell me what you want."

She whined, and Dylan's answering chuckle was enough to break through the lust. Drawing back, she rested her forehead against Dylan's. "I want more than this tiny little room can offer."

"I could make it work," Dylan said, lips trailing a path along her jaw. "Sit you up on that counter, haul down these yoga pants you love so much." They snapped the elastic fiber on her thigh, the pop going straight to Feb's already throbbing clit. "Eat the chef for a late-night snack."

Wet heat pooled between her legs. Shame that too, because now that Feb actually had a date for Valentine's

Day, she wanted to make the most of it. She playfully shoved Dylan back, a modicum of space between her body that was aching for release and the person she wanted to share that release with. "I did not need to know you were good with the dirty talk." Dylan's sly smirk and dark, heated gaze were almost her undoing, but Feb held firm. "And I want to hear more Tuesday night, but tomorrow, you're off."

Their brows drew together. "But it's prep day."

"Exactly. You know the menu, you know the drink." She flicked a glance at the empty glass, then back to the too-tempting bartender who'd concocted it. "Take tomorrow to take care of your family, then I'm going to take care of you and us Tuesday night. I want that date, Dylan," she said. "And everything that comes after, especially the snacks."

FIVE

Just as she exited the front of UTT each night, Feb entered the same way each morning. Cruising through her dining room and soaking in her concept and creation first thing reminded her why she was there and what she was doing. It calmed and centered her.

As she pushed open the front door on Valentine's Day morning, she needed that calming, centering effect more than ever. She was a ball of nerves over the evening service ahead and a live wire ready to spark over the date that would follow. Would the Render critic show? Would he give them a star-worthy review? Would everyone else dining with them tonight also enjoy their experience? Would she get to experience more than a heated make-out with Dylan after?

Even an extended session with her vibrator last night when she'd gotten home had failed to take the edge off, her dreams filled with parted lips, dirty words, and rosy pale skin. Not to mention sex on every surface—

A cleared throat interrupted her stroll down fantasy lane.

She glanced up.

Calm and centered vanished.

The large round table at the center of the dining room was occupied by a group of severe-looking individuals. Attractive, all of them, but also intense, their unfamiliar gazes focused on her.

Well, not entirely unfamiliar . . . "Dylan?" she said to her bartender and future date who was sitting directly across the table from where she'd entered, the center of the gathered group. "What's going on?"

"Jax," they replied.

Odd, but name preferences seemed the least of Feb's worries at the moment. "Okay, you want to go by your last name, sure . . ."

"Not my last name," Dylan said, holding her gaze. "Jax is my first name. J-A-X. And this is my family, some of them."

Feb swept her gaze left to right, trying and failing to see Dylan in any of the people on either side of them, but then she remembered how Dylan had been kicked out at home. How they'd landed in a shelter where they'd found their chosen family. But even then, the Dylan sitting at the table in their usual preservice nerd attire did not match the attire or attitude of the other people around the table. They looked far more like the Dylan that Feb was used to seeing behind the bar.

"Why don't you have a seat, Ms. Winters?"

Feb's gaze snapped to the Black woman to Dylan's left. She was the boss lady. Feb knew it the same way she immediately knew who was the head chef in any kitchen. The scary, hot blond in leather on Dylan's other side was also a boss lady. Maybe not in this particular instance, but an air of authority swirled around her too. And she seemed vaguely familiar? Hard to forget those ice blue eyes, the sharp lines of her dainty face, all that blond hair. Feb would swear she'd met her before. Had definitely seen her leather jacket on Dylan before. Had Dylan taken it? Was that what this was all about? Seemed a bit extreme, but so did these strangers.

She slid into the empty chair across from Dylan. "Are you in trouble?" she asked them.

"No, but I'm afraid you are. More than we intended." They averted their gaze, face angled away, but not before Feb caught the regret that streaked across it. Recognized it as the expression, the uneasiness that had weighed on Dylan the other day. Feb's stomach sank, then sank further as Dylan slumped in their chair, silent.

Boss lady took that as her cue. "I'm Melissa Cruz," she introduced herself. "And this is my work partner, Braxton Kane." She nodded at the white man on her left. He looked an odd combination of tired yet determined. He also kept a watchful eye on Dylan, and if Feb wasn't wrong, his hazel gaze was tinged with sympathy, his demeanor with protection. Given he looked around fifty, a father figure, maybe? Before Feb could ponder further, Melissa spoke again. "Jax works with me and Brax at Redemption Inc."

"And we're the rest of Jax's family," the scary blond said.

"Helena?" Feb said, the name coming to her out of a whiskey-soaked memory from that night after service when she'd wanted so badly to kiss Dylan. Dylan had put her in a car home instead—Helena's car.

"Good, you remember." Helena's smirk reminded Feb of a viper. Yeah, she was the scary boss lady. "Grumpy on the end over there"—she pointed at Brax—"is also my brother-in-law. Mr. Hair"—she pointed at the man to her right, who looked suspiciously like Mia Perri from AB's—"is my other brother-in-law, Chris. We're here for Jax, and we also have an interest in the target."

"What *target*?"

"Jacob Pappas," Melissa answered.

"The Render critic."

"Is a cover," Dylan said, reentering the chat.

"Right, I explained—"

"Pappas *is* a cover," Dylan said with a grimace. "So is his gig as a Render critic."

Feb propped her elbows on the table, chin in her hands, holding up her very confused head. "I'm sorry, I haven't had enough coffee yet for this conversation."

Dylan pushed back from the table, the scrape of their chair over the cement floor loud in the otherwise quiet space. They circled the table to Feb's side. "We're bounty hunters," they said. "That's what we do at Redemption, and Pappas—the person he *really* is—is wanted by numerous parties."

"Who is he?"

"It's safer if you don't know."

She scrubbed her hands over her face, hoping the What-The-Fuck of this all would be gone when she dropped her arms. No such luck. The four intense strangers were all still there. And so was Dylan—no, *Jax*—beside her. Not a stress dream, then. Definitely not a fantasy. This was reality, which brought a whole bunch of stress-inducing complications. "So, what?" she said, glancing up at the person she thought she'd known. "UTT V-day is off now?"

"No," Jax said. "We want you to go forward with the dinner." They sounded as unenthused about that plan as Feb felt.

Melissa pitched harder. "We haven't been able to pin down Pappas's location until now. This is the best shot we've had at him. That anyone has."

Feb slumped in her chair, gaze still on Jax standing beside her. "I should've never decided to do V-day."

"Probably not," they said with a wry half-smile. "But the Pappas thing is likely just bad timing. He's a foodie. You're a star. You and UTT were on his radar."

Feb glanced around her dining room, imagining it later tonight, full of diners, servers, and chefs. "Will my people, my guests be safe?"

"My husband will be in the kitchen," Chris spoke for the first time, his voice low and rumbly and with the local accent San Franciscans didn't think they had. "Put him on prep. He's good with a knife." Helena elbowed him in the side, earning her a shit-eating grin before he turned his attention back to Feb. "He can blend in and protect that area."

"One person?"

"Hawes will do the job."

"The rest of us will be out here," Helena said.

"But there are no resos left," Feb said.

"We paid off your diners."

Spluttering, Feb could hardly manage embarrassment. Panic crawled up her throat and strangled her voice. "How do you know they weren't critics?"

"*I* know," Jax said. "I hacked the critics' identities and

moved them to earlier seatings. Every real guest, including critics, will be cleared out of here by the time Pappas arrives."

"You should also give your servers the night off," Brax said. "For their safety."

Feb opened her mouth to protest, but Jax anticipated her objection. "Tell them they'll be paid," they said, "but that the chefs will serve dishes tonight. You've done that before for special dinners."

Feb scoffed. "And how are you going to keep my chefs safe? Or fool them into thinking you're real diners?"

"We'll be ready," Melissa said with a smile. "We're not only bounty hunters. Some of us like to eat too."

Undeterred, the panic expanding around Feb was a tough balloon to pop. Eyes scrunched closed, she rubbed them with her balled fist and shook her head. "This is all just a bad dream."

"'Fraid not, babe," Jax said as they laid a hand on her shoulder. "Take a deep breath." When Feb struggled, Jax squeezed her shoulder. "Try again, with me."

When she'd managed three, Feb opened her eyes and asked the person beside her, "Is Pappas worth this? Really?" Jax, of all people, knew Feb was sticking her neck out with this meal, that she'd put the kitchen through hell the past week. And now Jax and these people were adding a whole other layer of complication—of actual danger—on top of an already stressful situation. "I can't risk them," she pleaded with Jax. "I can't risk this."

"I know how much this place, your people, your reputation mean to you." They kneeled, hand on her bouncing knee. "Trust me."

"How?" Feb croaked. "I don't even know you."

Pain streaked across Jax's face, mixed with the earlier regret, but a blink later they locked it down. Raised their chin and tangled their fingers with hers. "Yeah, Feb, you do."

———

"And that's the last first seating served!" Lacey said as she twirled her way back into the kitchen, serving tray empty but for the smoke wand and glass dome they were using for tonight's apple crostata with burnt sugar glaze.

Everyone cheered, a few others danced at their stations too, the kitchen heaving a collective sigh of relief. Everyone except Feb, who stood near the freezers at the back. She glanced at the clock; half past eight. Pappas—or whatever his name was—would arrive within the next half hour.

In the dining room, Jax's colleagues had been steadily trickling in, Feb noticing them each time she delivered a main course to one of the real diners in the early seatings. Chris and Mel had arrived first, then Brax and Helena, then a few other folks who Jax had showed her photos of that afternoon. The last real diners would be finishing soon, the tables turning over for the second seatings. Everyone left in the dining room would be fake diners. Maybe Feb would feel some relief, then. As her gaze swept across the kitchen, she called that lie for the bullshit it was. Who was she kidding? Between her staff and the space itself, too much was still at risk.

Including Jax.

Adi waved from where she stood across the kitchen at the expeditor station. "Breathe, chef," she teased with a smile. "This is going smoother than we expected."

"No shit," Chloe said. "The single reservations keep things moving."

"And you've been kicking ass on the sauces," Adi commended her.

"She's right," Feb added. "Good job, Clo." She'd seemed nervous at first when Feb had put her on the line as saucier after Juan had called out sick, but she'd risen to the task.

As had Helena's brother, Hawes, who the rest of the kitchen thought was a temp she'd called in on the good word of Amanda and Justin. To most eyes, he was a natural in the kitchen, the sharp-featured man with light brown hair and chilly blue eyes the definition of meticulous. His prep station was pathologically neat, his knife work impeccable, his speed at tweezer-plucking herb leaves off sprigs frightening. He was friendly enough, efficient and deferential, all qualities you'd expect of the new person in any kitchen. But Feb saw what her other chefs missed—Hawes regularly glancing up to survey the space and the people in it, the tic of his jaw as he resisted giving orders, the way he'd rub his ear and angle his face away, speaking to their team through the in-ear comm Feb knew he wore.

Feb had refused the comm Hawes had offered her. She needed as much of her attention as she could wrest control of on the kitchen. Assessing each station, she deduced from there where things stood in the dining room. Pappas would be one of the last two seatings at nine. Before that, two others would arrive at quarter till. And the diners who'd arrived at twenty-five and were now arriving at thirty-five would have their tickets in shortly. Only six tickets left to cycle through.

"Tell them to go," Hawes said as he passed her on the way back from the pantry. "As they finish up."

"Read my mind," Feb said.

He smirked and the resemblance to his sister's crooked grin was uncanny, though less vipery on him. Until he picked up the chef's knife at his station and sliced apples faster and thinner than should have been possible without a lifetime of training and practice. Maybe viper wasn't dangerous enough. Ignoring the reality careening out of control around her, Feb focused on the tiny piece of here and now she could manage. "Listen up," she said, voice raised. "We've got six more tickets coming in. As you finish those up, get out of here." Adi opened her mouth to object, but Feb raised a hand, forestalling her. "None of you were supposed to have to work tonight. Take the rest of it off."

"You don't have to do it all yourself," Lacey said.

"I won't be. Ja—Dylan and new guy will help me close."

"If you're sure . . ." Adi said, doubt swirling in her dark eyes.

Feb nodded. "I'm sure."

She still didn't look completely convinced, but Adi had worked with her long enough to know when her mind was made up. She seconded the call to the kitchen. "You heard the chef. When your courses are done, skedaddle."

Folks tried to hide their smiles, tried to hide the energy they turned back to their stations with, but Feb recognized the higher gear her chefs shifted into as they prepped their final courses. Recognized it too of the newest person on the line.

"Nice work," Hawes said as she wandered closer.

"I just want everyone out of here."

He flipped her a slice of apple with his knife. "We'll get them out safe and sound, and you too."

"So much for my date tonight," she said before biting

through the translucent-thin slice. "Your knife skills are incredible. What is it your side of their family does?" After her earlier near slip, Feb was careful not to use Jax's name, fairly certain Hawes would follow.

He chuckled. "Not half as good as Hena's," he said, avoiding the other part of her question. But not the first part of her grumble. "We are sorry about the date. We'll make it up to you."

"If I even still want to go on it . . ."

"This is a lot, I know." He scraped the rest of the slices into a bowl, added brown sugar and cinnamon, then gave the apples a toss. He stepped away to hand them off to Lacey, then, once back at his station, met Feb's gaze again. "But they're one of the good ones. You couldn't do much better."

Feb knew that about Dylan, but did she know that about Jax? She could give them a chance, give herself the opportunity to find out, but they'd lied to her the past three months. Burned her trust already. Perhaps not like others in the past —Jax wasn't going to steal her restaurant concept like Brett had—but stealing her heart . . . That was a definite possibility with the direction things had been going with Dylan. The attraction was there physically, and Feb had also been attracted to the person she'd been getting to know. How much of that person was really Jax?

A question for another day because judging by Jax's posture as they appeared at the kitchen entrance—shoulders reared back, eyes frantically searching, hand lifting then stopping short of running over their head—there was a bigger problem here and now. Their gaze found her and Hawes, and for a moment, it looked like they were going to take off at a sprint toward them, until they seemed to remember the rest of the kitchen. They reined in their obvious panic and slowed their steps, the latter enough for Adi to catch them on their way past and offer a bite of crabby morel. Smiling, they popped it in their mouth, then continued to where Feb and Hawes stood at his station. "Pappas is here early," they said.

"How many real diners are left?" Hawes asked. He lined his knives up on a cutting board as if he were about to clean them. Feb didn't think so.

"Two," Jax answered.

Feb jerked her gaze to them, the math not adding up. "There should be three," she said. "The younger man in the wine-red jacket by the window, the midthirties person at the two-top near the front, and the blond middle-aged guy in a suit at the center round."

"The last one is with us," Hawes said.

Jax grimaced. "And Pappas sat right down at his table."

"Who is he?" Feb asked.

"SFPD. And Pappas's ex-husband."

Unlike earlier in the day, this time Feb let her curse slip . . . "What the ever-loving fuck?"

SIX

Jax should have composed themselves better before barreling into the kitchen, wide-eyed and alarmed. While the rest of the hyperfocused chefs hadn't noticed them, Feb, standing across the kitchen next to Hawes, had spotted them right away. Too fast for Jax to hide their distress, which only stoked Feb's higher. Jax hated heaping more on her, both in that instant and in the larger scheme of things, but hiding their own mounting stress wasn't natural either. They were still getting used to this whole undercover gig. They were a hacker, the one usually behind the computers running comms, all the stress and fear that came with an op channeled into keystrokes and commands. Working under-cover, in the very middle of the situation, effectively running point on an op, was new. And boy were they doing a bang-up job of it. First time out and said op was going sideways—and they'd fallen for a civilian bystander.

Though Feb wasn't just any civilian. She was a leader, like Hawes and Helena, like Mel and Brax. She was worried about her people and the restaurant she'd fought tooth and nail for, the reputation she'd built. She was the kind of person anyone would be lucky to spend more time with; she was *the* person Jax wanted to get to know better, to maybe build something more with when this was all over.

Which meant they had to pull their shit together, for Feb and for the future Jax wanted the opportunity to explore with her. They took a deep breath like Holt had taught them all those years ago at the shelter, a trick he'd learned from Brax years before in the military, then continued with the game plan the operatives in the dining room were ready to execute. "Mel signaled for evac," they told Hawes. "I already texted Holt."

"Yoo-hoo," Feb said, waving a hand between them. "Did you miss the question mark at the end of my WTF freak-out?" Feb split a glare between them and Hawes. "What the hell's going on?"

"The fire alarms in the building are about to go off," Hawes said as he stashed knives in the pockets of his chef's coat. "I'll make sure everyone back here is out. Our people will do the same with the couple remaining guests out front, if they haven't already."

Stepping closer, Jax gently clasped her wrist and waited for her to focus on them. "We're gonna end this now, Feb. Trust Hawes to take care of things back here. I'll make sure everything out front is taken care of too."

Her wary gaze was still locked on Jax's when the fire alarm began to wail.

"Get to your position," Hawes said to Jax, then raised his voice for the suddenly chaotic kitchen to hear. "Everyone out the back door!" he shouted, and all heads turned in his direction. "Let's go!" Granted, he was the new guy there, but Jax had met few people who questioned

Hawes when he broke out the king voice. Feb's kitchen staff was no exception, all of them flicking off burners, then hustling toward where Hawes was waving them to the back door.

All of them except Feb, who remained frozen in place, her frame practically vibrating, her gaze inching past worry to terrified. Jax shifted their grip, tangling their fingers with Feb's and giving them a squeeze. "Go, babe. I've got this."

She blinked away a smidge of worry, making room for the ounce of resolve she needed to be UTT's head chef. Nodding, she returned Jax's gesture, her fingers briefly squeezing around Jax's, before she headed Hawes's direction, ushering folks from behind. "You heard the new guy! Let's go, let's go, let's go!"

With Feb out of the line of fire, Jax raced back the opposite direction, pulling up short at the breezeway espresso station, just shy of the dining room entrance. In front of them, a standoff had ensued. Ariel Camino stood in the center of the room, a compact wall of muscle, his biceps bulging where they circled his leaner, taller ex-husband's shoulders, holding him to his front. Mel stood across the large round table from them, the rest of the hunters and operatives fanned out behind her, all of them at the ready, weapon of choice in hand, none of them guns—standard operating procedure for the Madigans and Redemption Inc.

Versus Ariel's Sig Sauer pressed against Fletcher's side.

Jax surveyed the room once more, searching for any guests and finding none. Good; the team had gotten them clear. They moved to step forward, then paused, motion at Helena's side halting their stride. Five fingers spread, twice in quick succession; Helena's signal for *under control*. Jax failed to see how, but in this situation, they were the least experienced of anyone in the room. Following Helena's order, they stepped into the shadowed coffee nook, grabbed a gasket removal awl, and listened while negotiations continued to play out in front of them.

"I'm sure we can work this out," Mel said.

"How?" Ariel scoffed. "I just wanted to eat a good meal, get what I came here for, and leave without anyone the wiser. But you screwed with the reservations, so the person I needed came and went already." He angled his face into Fletcher's, growling against his cheek. "You always screw up the plan."

"Let us bring you in," Fletcher pleaded in a voice far softer, more urgent than Jax had ever heard from the typically measured man. "We can protect you, Leo."

Whether he noticed it or not, Ariel drew Fletcher closer, grasping at warmth, at hope, in direct contrast to the cold, bitter laugh that fell from his lips. "Do you have any idea how many people are after me, cariño? How many people in your own station will try and slit my throat?" His chin jerked up, attention snapping to the door as Hawes slipped inside, a knife in hand. "Or maybe you'll beat them to it."

"You hurt any of my family," Helena said, "and we just might."

"Hena," Hawes cautioned, even as he firmed his grip on the santoku.

"Whose bounty are you collecting?" Ariel asked. "The CIA's or my family's?"

"Your family thinks you're dead," Mel replied.

"Not all of us," came a familiar voice from farther down the breezeway.

Spinning, Jax slapped a hand over their mouth to stifle their horrified gasp. Juan was walking up the short hall from the kitchen, Feb held to his front in a chokehold, similar to how Ariel was holding Fletcher, only Juan was taller than Feb and his gun was pressed to Feb's temple.

Jax wanted to dart out from their hiding spot, wanted to tear Feb from Juan's arms or at least catch her gaze and offer some comfort. Feb was shaking like a leaf, tears streaming down her cheeks, flowing freely out of wide, terrified eyes. But Jax had watched enough of these scenarios go down to know that they were in prime tactical position. Hidden in shadow, ready to intercept when the time was right, which would be any second at the rate Juan was closing in, his gaze locked on Ariel.

"Cousin," he practically spat, the hard, nasty edge in his voice far removed from the genial saucier Jax had gotten to know the past three months. Nothing in his background checks had indicated he was Camino cartel, but glancing between him and Ariel, there was no denying the resemblance between the two men. The same build, the same dark curly hair, eyes the same shape and, Jax guessed, the same light brown if Ariel were to pop out the contacts that made his black. "How'd you know?"

"Wherever he is"—Juan cut his gaze to Fletcher—"you're never far behind. And you're addicted to this shit." He gestured at a plate of food on a nearby table, the very dish Juan was supposed to help prepare tonight.

"I'm not going back," Ariel said.

In his arms, Fletcher shifted his gaze directly to Juan's side, to the spot where Jax was hidden, as if he were looking right at them and, with his hand trapped at his side, tapped a spot on Ariel's thigh.

Message received.

"That's fine with us," Juan said, removing the gun from Feb's temple and aiming it at Ariel.

"Now, Jax!" Helena shouted, and Jax darted out from their hiding place. With their left hand, they planted the awl directly into Juan's thigh, right where Fletcher had indicated. Juan howled, gunfire blasting, shiplap splintering—and his hold on Feb loosening enough for Jax to grab her and spin her free, the two of them sliding under the nearest table.

Chaos erupted around them—gunfire, hand-to-hand combat, furniture cracking, shouts for backup and handoffs—but Jax's sole focus was the shaking woman in their arms. Feb was on the verge of hyperventilating, her breaths short, her chest rising and falling rapidly. Jax held her close with one arm and framed her cheek with their other hand, helping her focus. "Feb, look at me. I need you to breathe. I'm gonna get you out of here, but I can't do that if you pass out." She nodded, frantically, no closer to drawing a full breath. Jax took one of her hands and laid it over their chest. "With me, Feb." And regulated their own breathing enough to bring Feb's down a measure. "That's right, babe, just breathe."

Hard to do, Jax was sure, with what sounded like an action movie tearing up the place around them, Feb's carefully crafted dining room, her dream, the scene of destruction. "Whatever is going on out there," Jax told her, "it doesn't involve you, and it doesn't involve UTT. By the time you walk back in here, it'll be set to rights."

"How?" she squeaked out.

"Because that's what my family does." They leaned forward and pressed their lips to Feb's, a swift and firm kiss, before resting their foreheads together. "I promise."

A giant gasping breath later, Feb nodded. Finally.

"That's good, Feb. Now, give me a couple more of those," Jax coaxed, and while Feb took two more deep breaths, they peeked out from under the table, assessing their exit route. The action had moved more squarely into the room, leaving the path to the hallway and kitchen clear. "All right," they said as they turned back to Feb. "Path's clear to the breezeway. Keep low and tucked to my side. On the count of three."

Feb's eyes were still saucer-wide, but they weren't leaking tears anymore, and Feb was no longer jumping at every shattering piece of wood outside their bubble. "You ready?" Jax asked, and she nodded. Jax gathered her against their right side, away from the action, and on the count of three, they darted out from under the table and around the corner. The chaos faded behind them as Jax straightened, Feb's hand in theirs, and sprinted down the breezeway into the kitchen.

Only to be drawn up short by Chloe stepping out of the pantry, arm raised, gun pointed straight at them. Feb's "What the fuck?" would've made Jax laugh if not for the deadly serious expression on Chloe's face.

"I'll be taking you now," the line cook said.

Jax slid in front of Feb. "You can't have—"

"I'm not here for her. I'm here for you."

Wet.

Rough.

Insistent.

Furry?

The last sensation, among the others against Jax's cheek, nudged them out of their Feb-induced fantasies and toward reality, pushing them through the fog they'd been wading in the past hour.

Ariel Camino's voice at their side, urging "Muévete, Sugar," propelled them through it faster.

They planted an elbow in the soft surface beneath them and struggled to lever upright. A gentle, steadying hand landed on their shoulder. "Take your time," Ariel said. "I was talking to the cat, not you."

Jax fought against their seemingly weighted eyelids, wresting them open just in time to see a snow-white ball of fluff jump off the end of the couch with an offended *meow*. "There a Spice around here too somewhere?" they asked as they continued to work their way to vertical.

"There is," Ariel said, helping them. "The orange one that shares his one brain cell with all the other orange cats in the world." His easy, charming smile was so at odds with the man who'd held Fletcher hostage at UTT that Jax gave their head a hard shake, thinking maybe the fog was still clouding their mind.

Pain sliced through their head, disabusing them of that notion.

Once they were steady, Ariel withdrew his hand and settled back in the chair beside the couch. "Water and ibuprofen," he said with a jut of his chin at the coffee table.

Jax scooted to the edge of the couch, slowly so as not to amplify their headache and to assess whether they'd sustained other injuries. They twisted their back, shook out their arms, stretched their fingers and legs. All fine. Nothing wrong that they could detect, and nothing binding their limbs either. They swept their gaze around the immediate area—no weapons in sight, no other humans besides Ariel. Then scoped out the larger area—an open floor plan kitchen-dining-living area in what appeared to be a cozy, lived-in, ranch-style home. In the middle of the back wall, large sliding glass doors led to a fenced-in backyard, quiet this time of night.

The same night or longer? "How long have I been out?"

"A few hours." Meaning they hadn't gone far. "We're in San Jose," Ariel said, anticipating their next question.

"Shit," Jax cursed before throwing back three tablets and a gulp of water. "Have you been this close the entire time?"

"I travel a lot, but yes, this is home base." He shrugged. "Lots of people, international airport, great food."

At the mention of food, memories from a couple of hours ago flooded back to the front of their mind. Shattering, splintering sounds from the dining room, Chloe locking a shaking Feb in the pantry, a prick to Jax's neck before the world went dark.

"Feb? My family?"

"All safe. It wasn't my intention to harm any of them."

"Didn't look that way with Fletcher."

He cast his gaze, light brown behind a pair of tortoise-shell glasses, out the back windows, but not before Jax caught the sadness and longing that pinched his features, that leaked into his voice. "Especially not him." After a long moment, he cleared his throat and turned back to them. "It was meant to be a diversion, but then Juan showed up."

"What happened to him?"

"In custody. Not talking, I assume."

"So I was your target?" Jax asked, piecing together what Ariel was saying, their stomach twisting. Was the damage to UTT, all the stress they'd put Feb under more their fault than they'd even realized?

"Not originally," Ariel said. "But once I got to UTT and realized *my* original target was gone, I had to improvise. Saw you behind the bar, knew who you really were and that you'd be an even better hacker than the one I'd planned to woo home. I activated Chloe at that point."

Jax gulped more water, then set the glass aside and braced their elbows on their knees, staring at the confusing man beside them. He was the picture of calm, the definition of measured, but warm in a way Jax would bet had balanced out Fletcher's reserved frostiness. History aside, here in the present, they'd somehow become the target of their original target. That part was less confusing; hacking would be a whole lot easier than playing at undercover these past few months. But what did Ariel need them to hack? "For what?" they asked and, pushing their position, sensing Ariel was a reasonable man, one that would expect some level of negotiation, added, "And what makes you think I'll help you?"

He grinned, the crinkles at the corners of his eyes deepening. "One, because I'm going to write your girlfriend a glowing review. And two, because when this is over, I'll turn myself in. You can take me to Isaiah yourself."

That was their second question answered, the terms more than acceptable to Jax. So what about the first? "And why do you need a hacker?"

"Because I want to know who inside the CIA set me up and sold me out to my family."

———

Jax started a new batch of searches running, then leaned back in the dining chair they'd occupied the past few hours, stretching out their fingers and cracking their knuckles.

"Ready for a snack?" Ariel said from the kitchen behind them.

Despite the late hour, he'd been the consummate host, keeping their mug full of coffee and cooking up something full of tomato goodness. The crack of eggs ten or so minutes ago, followed by the groan of the oven door, was a dead giveaway as to the dish, and Jax was more than ready for it. They set the laptop out of the way, searches still running, and moved the trivet Ariel had placed on the table to the center. "Bring over that shakshuka."

Ariel appeared at their side with a still-bubbling skillet of eggs poached in spicy tomato sauce. "Way to ruin the surprise."

"This is one of Feb's go-to dishes. I'd know that smell anywhere."

Ariel handed them bowls and silverware, then went back for the coffeepot, topping off their mugs while Jax dished out food. "I've had this dish all over the world," he said. "And people eat it at all different times. Breakfast, lunch, snack, dinner."

"Well, three in the morning seems as good a time as any."

They dug in, impressed at the depth of flavor Ariel had managed to get out of the canned tomatoes, punching them up with fresh ground spices and herbs he'd fetched from the yard. Helped too that Jax was starving. They'd missed lunch and dinner the day before, their stomach tied into too many knots to eat. They were still worried about the fallout at UTT, about how Feb was handling everything that had transpired, the WTF world she'd been tossed into, but Jax trusted their family to take care of her and UTT. They had to because this was where Jax was needed most: helping Ariel so they could get that Render review for Feb, complete the mission for Redemption, and bring Fletcher some closure—or a new beginning. The past few hours of hacking had also re-centered them, had renewed the confidence that the past few months undercover had chipped away at. Everyone had a particular skill set, and sneaking through firewalls was theirs.

"So, why did February Winters finally decide to do a Valentine's dinner?" Ariel asked as he spooned a second helping into his bowl. "First one since UTT opened."

Speaking of skill set . . . "You've been following her?"

"In the culinary world, yes," he said. "I am a foodie, that part's real, and she's an up-and-coming star. I also dined at the place she cheffed at before Under the Table. You could tell she was talented."

"She likes a challenge," Jax said. "If you followed her in the foodie news, then you've seen the headlines. The critics didn't think she could do it." Jax turned up their two middle fingers like Feb was so fond of doing. "She wanted to prove them wrong."

Ariel laughed, then settled back in his chair, bowl lifted as he tilted it this way and that, getting every bite. "I thought maybe you had something to do with it. That she was feeling the romantic spirit."

"She's not my girlfriend."

"You'd like her to be."

Jax shoved another spoonful into their mouth instead of answering.

"I also worked for the CIA. The connection between you

two was obvious in the less than five minutes I saw you together in the dining room." Finished with his food, he set the bowl aside. "Chloe filled me in too."

"Where is the little traitor?"

"In a safe house, for now. Once we're done, she'll be on her way to her dream job in Paris. Another Render-starred kitchen."

Finished, Jax stacked their bowl in Ariel's. "So she is a real chef?"

"She is, and I was able to give her something she wanted. It's a whole lot easier to get people to do what you want when you can return the favor." He carried their dishes to the sink, then returned with a pen and notebook. The leather journal with a sugar skull design embossed on the front looked well-traveled and well-used, the leather supple, the spine cracked, random slips of paper tucked between pages. Sliding into his seat, Ariel removed the elastic holding the bulging notebook together and opened to a blank page toward the back. "Now, if I'm gonna do this favor for you, I'll need you to fill in some details since my dinner was cut short. Let's start with how the V-day concept came about, beyond just . . ." He flipped his two middle fingers up, as Jax had done earlier. Jax had to admit, he was a charming kidnapper. And they enjoyed regaling him with the story of how solo resos, only local, and no pink had come about.

"That's fabulous," he guffawed, furiously scribbling notes. "If I'd gotten to eat, what would you have recommended?"

"Well, every table started with sumac and chili roasted chickpeas, which, in fairness, was Chloe's dish. For a starter, I'd rec the winter citrus salad. Beets, blood orange, and fennel with a toss in cumin-spiked olive oil and a sprinkle of pomegranate seeds." Jax fondly remembered the thirty-minute face-off between Adi and Feb over whether the blood oranges were pink or not. A couple of hours in the blast chiller had fixed that. "The brightness works to wake up the palate, the cumin acts as a bridge between the sumac and the next dish, and it worked with the Blue Rose drink that started the meal."

"Tell me about that."

They left out the personal connection both they and Feb had to the drink, instead describing how they'd adapted it from a Texas favorite, how there were nonalcoholic versions, and how the drink paired well with the first course.

"For a midcourse, you'd want to order the crab-stuffed morels, and Feb would be watching for your reaction from the breezeway espresso station. She damn near had a break-down over your mentions of morels in past reviews and how much was the right amount, so you better fucking rave about the ratio being just right."

"Noted," Ariel said with a grin.

Jax was fairly certain they'd given away more than intended—especially in light of his earlier girlfriend comment—but the morel dish was important to Feb. Ariel needed to know that. Before he could question further, Jax went on to describe the main dish they'd choose for him—pan-seared swordfish served with blistered vegetables and salmoriglio sauce. A hearty fish, moist and firm, a less fishy-tasting palate that would allow the charred veggies and bright herby sauce to shine. "And to finish," they said, winding down to the close, "the pomegranate chia pudding."

Ariel cocked a dark, bushy brow. "Not the smoked apple crostata? I saw it go by on my way in. Looked pretty cool."

"It was, and delicious too, but the pudding is a better bookend to where you started. The pomegranates come back and shine, and given the spices in that shakshuka, I think you'd enjoy the chai."

He scribbled another few lines, filling the remainder of a third page of notes, then closed the journal. "How many times did you go over that ideal progression with Feb?"

"At least a dozen."

"And how many people ordered it like that?"

Jax shot him a dirty look. "One." They held their stern glare for all of two seconds before they cracked up laughing alongside Ariel, their hilarity only subsiding when the computer running searches pinged. "Time for me to get back to work."

"You have enough food?" Ariel said as he stood.

"Plenty, thank you." Jax polished off their coffee and handed him the mug. "Everything was delicious."

He moseyed back to the kitchen to wash dishes while Jax waited for browser windows to fully load. Their gaze strayed to the notebook Ariel had left on the table, to the calavera stamped into the leather on the front. It had seemed generally familiar before—they'd attended more than a few of San Francisco's Day of the Dead festivals— but Jax had seen this particular design in a much different, closer context. "Did you give Fletcher the nesting doll? The sugar skull one?"

Silverware clattered in the stainless steel sink, and in the reflection on their monitor, Jax watched as Ariel leaned his weight against the edge of the sink, his head bowed and shoulders slumped, like his knees had completely given out from under him.

"It's on his desk," Jax said. "Has been since the day he joined the department."

"Jax—"

"I know what I saw in those five minutes too." And it sure as hell wasn't closure.

SEVEN

If Brax hadn't paused mid-opening the pantry door to announce his presence, he would have gotten a cast iron skillet to the face for the attempted rescue. But he had—"February, it's Brax. I'm gonna open the door now. It's all over. It's safe to come out."—and relief had flooded through her. And the tears had flooded out, impossibly more, as she'd fallen into his arms, the whole situation more than her tired, overworked, reality-stretched brain could comprehend.

Bounty hunters, secret identities, and hostages.

Knives, chair legs, and awls used as weapons instead of their intended purposes, in a restaurant at least.

Her restaurant. The scene of a Valentine's Day massacre.

Whose life had she stepped into? Because it sure as fuck wasn't her own, except that whole Valentine's-Day-is-cursed thing. *That* was her life, no doubt, but the rest of it . . . Mind still blown, and not in a good way.

And despite Brax's comforting words in the moment, it

wasn't all over. Jax was missing, so were Juan and Chloe, and across the foyer from where Feb sat in the more-than-she-could-afford-in-a-lifetime living room of the Madigan's Pacific Heights mansion, Helena, Hawes, Chris, and Brax stood around the long wooden dining table. With them was the other hostage from the scene, the SFPD detective who'd introduced himself as Isaiah Fletcher, the current chief of police, a pair of FBI agents, a US attorney, and Mel. No one had been killed, remarkably, but the gunfire, missing persons, and destruction of property had warranted law enforcement at the scene. More than just Fletcher, as everyone called him, and Feb kept hearing the group mention the CIA, which by their tone, no one around the table was keen to involve.

Not Feb's problem. She had a wrecked restaurant to sort out once she determined the full extent of the damage. From under the table, the skirmish had sounded like a nightmare—furniture splintering, glass breaking, plates shattering. When she'd emerged from the pantry, the battle was over, but the aftermath hadn't sounded much better, the crunch of boots over debris haunting her brain like a bad dream. One without visuals, Brax having ushered her out the back door and into a waiting SUV without a look back. A not small part of her wanted to duck out right now and go see the destruction for herself. Surely the gathered group had more important things to worry about than her. Maybe they wouldn't even notice her leave. Not leaving through UTT's front door was gnawing at her gut.

But so was her worry over Jax, growing with each hour that passed. Clearly her bartender was more than a mixologist. Between the folks they associated with and the way they wielded that awl, Jax was probably better than the average person at taking care of themselves; that didn't stop Feb from worrying. She was heartened that everyone else in this house seem equally concerned for them. But did Feb want any part of everyone else in this house? This was the family Jax had chosen and who'd chosen them—they were a package deal—but after tonight, Jax's family scared Feb more than a little. Feb sensed, however, that they were the people most likely to bring Jax home safe and sound. Which kept Feb from running out the door.

For now.

"It's February, right?"

Feb swung her gaze from the dining room to the brunet leaned against the kitchen doorjamb at the other end of the living room. Two mugs in hand, she wore a faded plaid robe, her hair in a messy braid over one shoulder, her features strikingly familiar—olive skin, dark eyes and hair, tall and gorgeous. Feb glanced again at the group in the dining room, Chris in particular.

"My brother," the woman said, confirming what Feb suspected. She crossed the room and held out one of the mugs to Feb. "London Fog. My daughter says you're a fan."

More of the resemblance resolved. "Mia? From AB's?"

"That's the one," the woman said with a smile as she lowered herself next to Feb. "I'm Celia. Mia's mom and Helena's wife."

Feb whipped her gaze back to the dining room, trying and failing to make sense of the ice-cold, scary boss lady dressed in leather married to Queen Cozy sitting beside her, Celia's clean, fresh face and easy smile warmth personified.

Celia chuckled. "Yeah, I wasn't sure at first either when I met her over my brother's hospital bed."

Feb nearly spilled her drink. "I bet that's a story."

"You have no idea, but it worked out in the end, for both of us."

With the added context, Feb sipped her drink and surveyed the living room again, seeing more of the family who lived here beyond just the initial impression of extreme wealth. A slew of framed family photos on the walls and mantel, stained-glass lamps that cast the room in soft, warm colors, cat beds by the fireplace, plushie toys, Legos, and picture books overflowing various bins around the room. "You two have more kids?"

"My son, Marco, who's in high school. The toys are Lily's, Holt and Brax's daughter, for when she stays here. Holt has an office upstairs." Celia lowered her voice, a conspiratorial whisper. "Don't tell my wife, but Lily's the real queen of this castle."

Feb giggled into her mug, the mental image of Helena bowing to whatever toddler ruled these parts hilarious. It was a much-needed release from the heaviness of the past however many hours since Feb's life had veered into the absurd.

Celia smiled softly and patted her knee. "For what it's worth, I hid out here after my garage was shot up." Feb swung her wide-eyed gaze back to Celia. "Trial by fire, it's the Madigan way, and you're handling it well." She withdrew her hand and rose. "They're good people, and Jax is one of the best."

Her parting words led Feb's thoughts back to her missing . . . Bartender? Colleague? Friend? Something more? Jax had been an indispensable member of the UTT team the past three months—a fixture behind the bar and the key to a smoothly operating front of house. They were an easy fit in the kitchen too. Downright essential the past week, as they'd taken Feb's fuck-you V-day wild hair and helped turn it into a menu Feb was proud of. And when Feb's perfectionist streak had threatened to upend the entire V-day effort, Jax had held her together, giving her a couple hours' peace to recenter herself. And last night, when V-day had gone off the rails, exactly like Feb had feared, Jax had worked with Hawes and the rest of their team to make sure her people were clear and safe. But before those alarms had started wailing . . . Feb and her team, Jax included, had been kicking ass, executing their V-day concept to perfection. Would all that hard work be lost now? Buried under a sea of headlines about the unexpected evacuation and melee that had ensued? No Render review and no stars by the front door, if there even still was one. No date with the alluring bartender—bounty hunter—who had captured her attention and had been thawing her heart, little by little each day.

Cursing, she set her mug on the floor between her feet, propped her elbows on her knees, and scrubbed her hands over her face. Went to rub her eyes, then, remembering her contacts were still in, stopping at the last second with more muttered *fucks*.

"That doesn't sound or look good," Brax said, his voice and footsteps echoing as he crossed the massive foyer to her.

She raked her fingers through her hair and clasped it with both hands behind her neck, stretching her aching muscles as she glanced up at the tall, spindly man. He looked as tired as Feb felt. "Do I want to know what my restaurant looks like?"

"Currently, no," Brax said, perching on the arm of the couch closest to her. He ran a hand over his close-cropped hair, and Feb at once knew where Jax had picked up the habit. "But next time you see it, it'll look just like it did at the start of the evening."

"That's what Jax said."

"Trust us."

"That's what Jax said too, then all hell broke loose." She let go of her hair and dropped her arms, letting her forearms and hands dangle between her knees. "What are you gonna do to get them back?"

"The feds and SFPD are putting out APBs on Ariel and Chloe. Juan is in custody but not talking. We're going back through everything on Ariel Camino and his aliases to find where he might be hiding out."

There was that word again—*alias*—the precise language that Jax had used and that all made sense now. Feb hung her head, more of the pieces coming together, all of it too heavy.

Brax coasted a hand across her back, over her shoulders. "We're working on it, and my husband is upstairs now monitoring web traffic. Jax knows to get us a message in these situations." He squeezed her shoulder and waited for her gaze again. "The question is, once they do, if we need your help, are you in?"

———

"So I just hit this button?" Feb lightly brushed the Return button on the far-right keyboard, one of three ergonomic monsters that glowed with rippling rainbow lights, all of them wireless and situated in a line on the wall-length desk below a massive bank of monitors.

"Yep!" said the preschooler with a headful of ginger curls beside her. "Then you on that screen." Lily pointed to the eye-level monitor directly in front of Feb before flopping back in the gamer chair that was fourteen sizes too big for her. From her other side, Holt handed his daughter a crocheted blanket, a coloring book, and a box of crayons, like they'd done this dance countless times before. Same with the video calls, Feb guessed, given Lily's precise instructions.

"Who do you call on this thing?" Feb asked.

"I call David every weekend."

"Who's David?"

Her freckled cheeks flamed as red as her ringlets. "He has red hair like me. Texas his other daddy now."

Feb tried to make sense of *Texas* as a father until she recalled her conversation with Jax about the blue rose cocktail, particularly when and where Jax had first tried it. "You mean the family friend from Texas?"

"Marsh," Holt said with a nod. "He lives in San Diego now with his husband, Levi, and Levi's son, David." He ruffled Lily's curls. "Though we call other folks in Texas too, don't we?"

"Mama Mila and Irina." Clapping, Lily bounced in her chair, the crayons and coloring book forgotten, tumbling to the floor with the blanket. "Can we call now?"

"Nice try, princess," Brax said as he appeared behind them and plucked Lily from the chair. She squealed in delighted surprise, wriggling in his arms until Brax situated her on his hip. "It's only Wednesday. You gotta be patient." She blew a raspberry at him, and Feb laughed out loud.

Holt too as Brax blew one back at their daughter. "I'm gonna take her down for breakfast," Brax said. "What can I bring you two?"

"Celia fed me already," Feb replied. She'd fallen asleep on the living room couch in the wee hours of the morning, lulled to sleep by the rumble of voices across the foyer and the two massive cats who'd made themselves at home on her feet. She'd roused several hours later when delicious aromas—fresh-brewed coffee, cinnamon rolls, eggs and cheese—had started wafting from the kitchen. "And I've had enough coffee for a week."

Holt laughed even louder than he had at his daughter's antics. "No such thing in this household." He tipped his head back to look up at his husband. "Refill, please?"

"Helena's rocket fuel?"

"Big mug."

Smiling, Brax leaned over and kissed his husband's forehead. Lily mimicked him, dropping a smacking kiss on her father's nose. "Anything else you need?" Brax said.

"Texas or Whiskey. Or Barbie." More code names, Feb assumed, all above her pay grade, though the last one made her giggle.

"I'll see who's available," Brax said before heading down the stairs from the third floor . . . Room? Command center? Lair? Celia had said Holt had an office upstairs, but this was more than a mere office.

Holt's domain in any event, the middle Madigan's fingers flying over the keyboard in front of him. He paused after an initial flurry of typing and reached for an earbud case. "I'll give you some privacy."

"Would you mind listening?" Feb asked, comfortable enough with the flannel-wrapped giant after the past half hour in his easy company. "After what happened with Juan and Chloe, I don't know who on my team to trust. Maybe you'll notice if something is off."

"I can do that." He shifted to the chair Lily had vacated, then used his mouse to drag his open windows of web searches and code to the monitors directly in front of him. His fingers flew once more, but the slight angle of his head, his lifted ear and split glance, indicated he was ready to be the impartial observer Feb needed.

She hit the Return button, joining the video chat she'd sent an invite for earlier that morning. Squares populated the screen, each one filled by a member of her kitchen staff. Everyone except Chloe and Juan.

And Jax.

Feb's audio connected and voices erupted all at once. Chefs talking over each other, speculating, then lobbing questions in her direction once they noticed her join. She waved a hand, and the chatter quieted. "Can everyone hear me okay?"

A chorus of "Yes, chef" echoed back, and it was the first time Feb had felt like herself since she'd walked into UTT yesterday morning.

Holt chuckled beside her.

She swatted his tattooed arm, then smiled and turned her attention back to her friends and colleagues. "Good. First, I want to thank everyone for an amazing service last night. Until that alarm went off, we were kicking serious ass."

"Yeah, we were," Adi said as she sipped from a mug on her South Beach balcony, the Giants' ballpark visible behind her.

"Most of our reviewers were in before we had to cut the

night short, so be on the lookout for reviews popping up online today. Text the group thread if we get some good ones. *Only* the good ones," she emphasized. She had enough terrifying and uncertain circumstances to deal with. She didn't need scathing reviews of their first V-day effort added to the seemingly insurmountable mountain.

"I haven't seen any coverage of what happened at the end," Lacey said.

"What did happen?" another chef asked.

"Where are Juan and Chloe?" from another. "Were they hurt?"

"Where's Dylan?" Adi said, her dark eyes narrowed. "Or the new guy? He was a pro last night."

Feb cleared her throat, knee starting to bounce under the desk. "They couldn't make the call, but they're okay."

"And you?" Lacey said. "Are you okay? I saw you go back in."

"I'm fine," she said. "I went for my grandma's skillet." Holt stifled another laugh. Brax must have told him how he'd found her in the pantry. "Then I stayed behind to speak with the authorities."

"And the restaurant?" Adi asked.

"Took some damage from an issue in the upstairs unit." The story she'd rehearsed with Brax and Hawes this morning. "We'll be closed through the weekend for repairs," she told them. "We should be back for prep on Monday and open again Tuesday, assuming everything's repaired by then."

"Is there anything we can do to help?" Lacey asked.

"Go to Tahoe or Napa, take a well-deserved vaca—"

"Holy shit!" Adi interrupted, standing abruptly, her head knocking one of the many hanging flowerpots on her balcony. She brushed dirt and hair out of her face, her gaze never leaving the phone screen, though to Feb, it didn't seem like her sous was actually looking at the camera. It looked like she was reading something instead. "Render review is up." She pumped her fist. "Three fucking stars!"

Feb muted her mic and whipped her gaze to the side. "How?"

"Is Dylan there with you?" Adi practically shouted, but Feb's attention was on Holt's screen, the Render review displayed there. After a moment, he rotated in his chair toward her, a wide grin splitting his freckled face. "There's a message for us. In the review."

———

"Guests don't usually wash dishes."

Feb glanced up from the soapy dishwater she was fore-arms deep in as Brax entered from the dining room, a collection of empty mugs dangling from his bent fingers. "I'm incapable of doing nothing in a kitchen. Drop those mugs in here," she said with a nod to the sink.

"Baba!" Lily shouted from the step stool beside Feb. "She got more tattoos than you or Daddy." In her excite-ment, she whacked Feb's inked biceps with the spatula she'd half dried, slinging water and laughter everywhere.

"Easy, princess." Brax slid the utensil from her tiny grip and set it on the island behind them. "As for the tattoos, Feb's a chef. Every one I've ever met has ink, even the cooks your Daddy and I knew in the army."

"Every chef I know too," Feb added. "We have an annual staff contest at Under the Table. Best new ink."

"I wanna be a chef," Lily declared with all the awe and certainty of a four-and-a-half-year-old.

"You wanted to be a bus driver last week," Celia said from the other end of the kitchen island where she was whipping up cream cheese frosting for the carrot cake she'd baked that morning.

In a flash, Lily swung from certain to uncertain, her expressive face on the verge of crumbling, the little girl torn between today's fascination and last week's wonder. Celia spared them the impending breakdown. "If you want to be a chef," she said, "come help me frost this cake."

"Frosting!" She raced down the two stool steps, surprisingly graceful for a preschooler, and to her aunt's end of the island, climbing just as gracefully onto the barstool beside her. Far more gracefully than Feb had ever managed, and she spent more than half her life these days around barstools.

Feb turned her attention back to the dishes and Brax, who'd picked up Lily's abandoned dishtowel. "I'm sorry," she said to Brax. "I'm not the best with kids. I didn't mean to give her—"

"Another career option? More glimpses of art?" Brax dried and tucked utensils away. "None of those things are bad for my daughter at any age."

He was a good dad, and so was Holt, their interactions with Lily this morning reminding Feb of the unconditional love her own parents gave her. She'd been ready to call them, to reassure them she was fine, if news had broken about the incident last night. But it mysteriously never had —or maybe not so mysteriously given the connections Jax's family seemed to have. She opened her mouth to ask Brax how they'd managed that feat, but Brax beat her to a more pressing question—the here and now. "I asked last night if you would be in if the time came we needed your help." He finished drying the last mug and handed her the dishtowel. "Well, the time's here. Are you in, Feb?"

As she dried her hands, Feb let her gaze wander from Celia pulling Lily's curls back so they wouldn't get in the frosting, to Brax's hazel eyes full of kindness and patience, to the tired, yet determined people in the dining room who'd worked all night and morning to find a way to bring Jax home. These were good people. And so was Jax, who was patient, funny, smart, an asset to UTT, and the person who had held Feb together the past week. Jax had given her more than only the next service to look forward to.

Her phone vibrated. She dug it out of her pocket and smiled as another rave review hit the UTT text thread. They wouldn't have any reviews, including the Render one, without Jax, who'd helped define the V-day concept and who'd reined in Feb when she'd almost ruined it all. This was Jax's victory too, and Feb wanted to celebrate it with them. She tucked her phone back in her pocket and met Brax's gaze. "I'm in."

Brax looped an arm around her shoulders, giving her a sideways hug before leading her into the dining room. Everyone's attention snapped their direction. Channeling some of Lily's grace, Feb managed to stay upright on wobbly knees as she crossed to the empty chair beside Hawes. "Is Jax okay?"

"They're good," Hawes said. "Unhurt. Hacking for Ariel."

"But he's the bad guy?"

Hawes tilted his head one way, then the other. "To be determined."

"I don't follow."

A deep, unfamiliar chuckle rumbled from the far end of the table. "It's not always easy." The honeyed Southern drawl drew Feb's gaze, but that sexy accent was just the tip of the iceberg. Its owner was attractive enough to sink the fucking Titanic—waves of light brown hair, bright blue eyes, a wide, easy smile that had no business existing in this world. And good god, those shoulders. "Jesus, you're fucking hot" was out of her mouth before she could catch it. She belatedly slapped a hand over her mouth, fingertips seared by the heat hitting her cheeks. "Sorry, sorry, sometimes the words outrun my brain. Apologies, mister . . ."

The unfairly handsome man smiled wider, humor dancing in his eyes. "Jamie's just fine."

Feb didn't think the rest of the table was snickering at Jamie. "What's so funny?" Besides the hotness iceberg sinking her manners. "I'm missing something, aren't I?"

"Not a sports fan?" Helena asked.

"I can't walk across my parents' backyard without falling into a hole, so no."

"Can we get back on topic?" The weariness in Fletcher's voice sucked the humor right out of the room. The detective looked weary too, his blond hair raked through, the stubble over his upper lip dense, his brown eyes impossibly more bloodshot than they were last night.

"Again, sorry," she apologized to the table at large, but mostly to him. "So Jax is okay for real?"

"For now," he said. "I don't think Ariel will hurt them. There's no evidence he ever hurt anyone."

Except you. The words were on the tip of her tongue, but she caught them this time, not wanting to burden the poor man any more. He'd been held hostage like her, and from what she'd overheard last night, he'd also run inter-ference with SFPD at the scene. And he'd had some sort of past relationship with Ariel. She didn't need to add to his burdens; he had plenty already. "That's good." She gave him a small nod, then, glancing around the table again, focused on Mel. "Umm, Brax said you needed my help?"

"We need you to redo the Valentine's Day meal."

Feb shot out of her chair so fast it fell over. "Nope, nope, nope."

Hawes clasped her wrist, more gently than she would have expected him capable of, enough to give her pause. "Hear us out," he urged. "I want to get Jax back safely as much as you do. We all do."

She held his ice blue stare, trying to soak up some of his steadiness. A deep breath later, she kneeled, righted her chair, and lowered herself back into it. "I'm listening."

Holt slid a printout across the table to her. She recog-nized the branded banner across the top, the headline and review she'd read at least a dozen times since it had appeared that morning. "Did you catch what Ariel said in the second to last paragraph?"

"That he'd be back this Friday. I figured it was filler, like all the rest, seeing as he didn't eat a bite to start with."

"We think it was meant to lure someone there," Mel said.

"So you—and now Ariel—want to use my restaurant as bait? Again?" She shook her head. "Nope, no thank you. I can't risk my people or guests like that again. Not to mention the problems of the bullet holes in the ceiling, furniture in splinters, knives in the upholstery . . ."

"We can fix the dining room by Friday," Brax said. "And

none of your chefs or guests would be there this time. Only us."

"We can handle the kitchen too," Mel said. Jamie barked out a laugh that he failed to cover with a cough, but Mel ignored him, her intense gaze still on Feb. "You don't need to risk yourself."

"Jax was risking themselves, though, weren't they? These past three months, Ariel could have come into UTT at any time. Jax was watching over us in case he did."

"They were," Mel conceded.

"I'll be there. It's my kitchen, and I owe Jax that much." She angled in her chair toward Hawes. "Can I get your help in the kitchen?"

While his smile wasn't as showstopping as Jamie's, its softness in a face of such sharp angles was equally beautiful and far more interesting. "I'd love the chance to cook with you again."

"Chloe will be there too," Holt said, and Feb nearly sprained her neck whipping her head around so fast. "Like I'm giving that bitch a knife ever again."

Laughter erupted around the table, even from Fletcher.

Still chuckling, Hawes bumped his shoulder against hers. "I'm better and faster than she is with a blade. Trust me."

Trust. She was in a room full of strangers, still unsure who were the good guys and who were the bad, but the one thing she was sure of was that she wanted to get Jax back.

"I'm trusting all of you," she said, gaze sweeping the table before landing back on the boss lady. "After that Render review, whether it was real or not, and after all the others that have come in, I need to be able to open my doors next week. This is the wave we've been waiting for, and I need to ride it, preferably without bullet holes in my ceiling this time. And I need my bartender back. I get that they have a job to do with you, but at least until I can find a replacement, Jax stays on at UTT, assuming they want to. Those are my conditions."

Mel stood, a hand stretched across the table to her, a smirk hitching up one corner of her mouth. "We have a deal, Ms. Winters." Shaking on it, Feb thought maybe, just maybe, the boss lady had recognized another in her too.

EIGHT

"Do you always eat in the middle of the night?" Jax asked as Ariel slid a steaming bowl of pho onto the table beside them. The noodle soup's gingery, beefy aroma woke the cat that had been snoozing in their lap the past few hours. More sleep than Jax had caught at any one time the past— they glanced at the time onscreen—fifty hours. The Friday deadline Ariel set had left them no choice but to hack all day and night for the answers he needed.

"Think of this time like that week between Christmas and New Year's, when conventional rules of society just disappear." He flitted his fingers in the air, and Jax laughed.

"There has not been nearly enough cheese for that comparison."

"Noted," he said, grinning as he carried his bowl to the adjacent den.

They hit Return, the final missive sent through layers of spoofed IP addresses. "Well, that's that," they said as they shooed Sugar off their lap before she got into their soup.

"You're either going to have a dinner party of many, of one, or of none."

"Let's hope for the right *one*."

They lifted their bowl of noodles, slurping a bite, and nearly groaned aloud. The soup tasted even better than it smelled. While the cheese had been absent the past two days, delicious dishes had not. From the first night's shak-shuka to tonight's soup, Ariel had fed them well—and kept them in good coffee. The benefits of being held captive by a foodie, though *held captive* seemed more a strong accusation than the truth. Jax was fairly certain they could've left at any time. They'd stayed for Feb, and for Fletcher, and because it was their job. And hacking was the part of it they could do.

"You know," Ariel said as he folded a leg under himself on the couch, "the Agency knows about you, your mentor, Holt, and your other associates, at Redemption and otherwise."

Translation: Madigans. "Of course they do." Jax angled in their chair toward them, bowl still in hand. "And the CIA can do nothing about us on US soil."

"No, that's for the FBI, which is in your pocket."

They shrugged. "Or we're in theirs. Po-tay-to, Po-tah-to."

He laughed, his smile transforming him into the charming man Jax had gotten to know a little, the one they could see bringing Fletcher out of his shell, until Ariel's gaze landed on the laptop and tension rushed back in. "Go over it again."

They took another slurp of soup, then set the bowl aside. Standing, they grabbed the laptop off the dining table and carried it to the den. After lowering themselves beside

Ariel, laptop balanced on their knees, they opened ten different CIA profiles. "These are the ten CIA employees who have had the most contact with the Camino cartel over the past five years." Another strike of the keys and half the photos disappeared. "These five are the ones I can prove took money from the cartel. May not have been intentional, or even knowing, but money flowed from point A to point B."

"I'm going to need that list to send to the Agency."

"You can hand it to Fletcher and the FBI yourself."

"I can live with that."

Two more keystrokes and only one person remained onscreen. "Officer Caleb Fitzpatrick, who was following you as you were following Fletcher. From Miami, to Boston, to California."

Ariel set his bowl on the coffee table. "He was on me before I even left Fletcher in Miami."

"Looks like it." Jax closed Fitzpatrick's CIA profile and brought up a running list of email addresses. "And these are all of his alias emails." Jax highlighted one midway down. "Including this one that subscribes to the Render RSS feed." They highlighted the last one on the list. "And this is the alias he used to feed the Agency that tip about you selling secrets."

"Fuck." He raked a hand through his short, dark curls. "It's gotta be him. That's too many dots connected."

Jax handed the laptop to Ariel and retrieved their bowl of pho. "Do you know him?"

Ariel clicked Fitzpatrick's photo forward again, took a good long look at him, then shook his head. "I've never seen this guy in my life. Don't even remember hearing his name."

"Why not just prove you didn't do it?" Jax asked after another few bites. They'd spent days finding the mole but in doing so had also turned up evidence to support Ariel's innocence. And while they barely knew the man, they were fairly certain he was innocent, on all counts. Guilty people didn't set themselves up to be caught so easily. "I can help you get whatever additional proof you need." Doing so would get them both what they needed. Redemption the bounty delivered; Ariel the evidence to refute the charges against him.

Ariel didn't buy it, his laughter cold and bitter like it had been the other night at UTT. "My last name is Camino. The Agency knows that—recruited me for it—but to them, it was only a matter of time." He set the laptop on the coffee table, then reached down to pet the orange ball of terror that wove around his ankles, sniffing for his bowl of barely touched soup. "Question is, why now? And why Fitzpatrick?"

"Money." The most obvious answer, but it was rarely all there was. Working at SFPD, then for the Madigans and Redemption had taught them that much. "Probably some sort of leverage at play too."

"Always a favorite with the cartel." He scooped Spice into his lap, his fingers carding through the cat's short orange fur, seemingly lost in a memory Jax didn't want to imagine. He came back to the present a moment later. "You found the money already. What about the leverage?"

They finished their last spoonful of soup, then gestured with their utensil at the laptop. "Still running searches." His gaze followed where they pointed, fixating on the picture of Fitzpatrick again. Jax raised another possibility that couldn't be ignored. "That officer was not the one at UTT

Wednesday night. Even though I funneled your review his way, we don't know if he'll be the one to show tonight either. Or—"

"It could be someone from my family. Like Juan."

"Do they want you back?"

Ariel shifted, lifting one hip and jostling Spice off his lap in the process, the orange cat screeching a *meow* of protest. Jax chuckled, but their amusement died when Ariel pulled a plain gold wedding band from his wallet and slipped it on his left ring finger. "They haven't wanted me since I put this on my finger."

The same gut punch they'd felt for Fletcher the other night resurrected itself again, hitting harder this time with the force of shared sympathy behind it, Jax understanding all too well being disowned for who they were and who they loved. Jax wondered about the latter between Ariel and Fletcher. "Do you want him back?"

"I never wanted to give him up." He stood before Jax could recover from another hit, even if they had suspected as much. "Your people got the message?" Ariel asked, giving them a professional hand up.

Recovering, they leaned forward and, with a couple of quick keystrokes, loaded the surveillance feed from inside UTT. After the review had been posted, they'd knocked at the secure network transmitting the surveillance feed, and Holt had opened a connection for them. They'd peeked in countless times the past two days whenever they'd needed a shot of purpose to keep them going with the endless hack. Even at this late hour, the construction crew Jax recognized from Hawes and Chris's home reno was busy finishing repairs, while other members of their family and Redemption were moving in furniture and putting the final touches on UTT. "They got the message."

Ariel wandered back into the kitchen, but Jax's gaze remained locked on the woman behind the bar orchestrating the madness. Hair in a topknot, dressed in jeans and a sweater, her sleeves pushed up to her elbows, her glasses sliding down her nose, Feb looked good, like everything Jax had ever wanted. They just hoped Feb still felt the same way about them when this was all over.

———

Approaching UTT's back entrance, Jax spared a glance and a two-finger wave for the camera they'd installed over the door last week.

We're a go, they mouthed to Holt, who was no doubt watching from behind a monitor in the surveillance van close by, monitoring every coming and going at UTT and in the surrounding area. Catching sight of the high-tech smart lock on the back door, they mouthed a *Thank you* to Holt too. The original single deadbolt had been the bare minimum; not nearly secure enough for Jax's liking. The new digital lock was a far better security solution and, at least for tonight, made it easier for Holt to let Jax in, the glowing keys turning from red to green.

They opened the door and stepped inside, the familiar aromas wafting from the kitchen at once comforting. The herby, minty richness of roast lamb, the deep, earthiness of morels and beets, the spicy brightness from the sumac chili chickpeas Feb had glommed onto, and the yeastiness of fresh baked bread. While Jax had been fed well the past few days, their stomach grumbled for more. And by the smell of it, Hawes was doing Feb proud, cooking in her stead with Chloe, whom Ariel had called back down from Napa.

They hung their overcoat, gloves, and beanie in their locker, then carefully unpacked their bag, using equal care to arm themselves with blades and brass knuckles tucked into leather pockets. Suited up, including the in-ear comm unit that had been waiting for them in their locker, they paused in front of the sink, checking their reflection in the mirror and finger-combing their freshly dyed pink mohawk back to spiked life. Time and best intentions had gotten away from them Tuesday. Today, they'd made sure to take the time to do Feb this honor for her bravery and cooperation this past week, for the place in her UTT family they'd made for Jax. It had also been worth it for how fast Ariel's eyebrows had raced to his hairline. Jax imagined Feb's reaction would be the same at first, then, once she recalled the promise Jax had made her, she'd snort a laugh at seeing that promise finally fulfilled. If Feb was sitting next to Holt in the van, maybe Jax would even hear her over the comms.

They were waiting for that snorting laughter through the comm as they stepped into the kitchen.

Only to hear it in person.

Across the kitchen, Feb stood in the aisle between the wall of ranges and ovens and one of the prep islands, hair up and chef's coat on, a baking sheet of fresh-from-the-oven chickpeas on the island in front of her. Her gaze, though, was locked on Jax, flicking back and forth between their face and hair, her smile growing impossibly wide. "You did it."

"You're not supposed to be here."

"Well, hello to you too." Her smile didn't dim, and neither did the determination Jax also recognized in her eyes. The last time they'd seen it there was Sunday night, when Feb had ordered them home to take care of their family so they could have their date Tuesday night after service. Late, like the hair, but right then, Jax wanted to make that date happen more than anything, even while the larger part of their brain was still screaming objections at Feb's presence tonight.

Hawes appeared at Feb's side, similarly coated. "She insisted on being here." He raised a hand midair, sprinkling salt on the chickpeas. "It's her restaurant."

His attempt to sprinkle reason on Jax's objections didn't work. Especially not with Chloe an aisle over, working the sauces. "But things could go sideways a million different—"

Hawes's "Maybe you two should talk" collided with Feb's "We should talk," and if Jax didn't know Hawes was gay and one hundred percent devoted to his husband, they might have been worried about how quickly Feb and the assassin-wannabe-chef had bonded.

Feb gave the pan of chickpeas a shake and, apparently satisfied, headed for her chef's nook, giving Jax no choice but to follow. As they passed, Hawes flipped up the tails of his black chef's coat, showing them the knives attached to his belt and the barrel shape of his garrote in his pocket.

Feb was likewise packing protection, a corkscrew and folding knife that she removed from her back pockets and placed on the counter before climbing onto her stool. Once settled, she rotated toward Jax, propped her heels on the stool's rung, knees spread, and beckoned Jax closer with a crooked finger.

"I'm sorry," Jax said, stepping the rest of the way into the nook but leaving some distance between them, giving

Feb space to take or leave their apology. "I didn't mean to say you can't take care—"

Feb apparently didn't need space, obliterating it instead. Grabbing them by the jacket lapels, she hauled them in for a kiss that was as determined as her gaze had been in the kitchen. Mouth angling over theirs, she demanded entrance, parting Jax's lips and diving inside with her tongue. Fingers traveling up Jax's neck, lifting goose bumps across their skin and sending heat and wetness arrowing south. Carding her fingers through their mohawk and skimming them over their freshly shaved sides.

Jax melted, giving Feb some of their weight and kissing her back with all the desire that had built the past few months, accelerated the past week by separation and admiration. Feb had challenged the critics with her V-day menu, living up to every bit of hype about her out there, and she'd met every challenge thrown her way, from the Render review news to a restaurant full of bounty hunters and assassins who'd carved up her pride and joy. But she'd bounced back, persevered each time, and after all of that, including Jax's part in the madness, she still seemed to want them.

They slid their hands up Feb's thighs, over the curve of her hips, then under her ass, hauling her to the edge of the stool, both of them gasping as they rocked their hips together. Fuck, they wanted to take her apart right here, and Jax thought maybe Feb would let them, judging by her moans, her hand roaming over Jax's sides and back, her hips continuing to rock.

But fuck, there was no door on this fucking nook, and if there was one thing Jax had learned from their years with the Madigans, it was that locked doors were a necessity.

The number of stories they'd heard about unfortunate interruptions gave them serious pause. As did Ariel's ETA, the vibrating phone in their pocket no doubt the thirty minutes out text they were expecting. Reluctantly, they pulled back and rested their forehead against Feb's, the both of them gasping for breath, Feb catching hers first. "I love the pink on you. I hate it in all other circumstances, but on you . . ." Her lips curved against Jax's. "You pulled it off."

"I owed you," Jax said as they drew back enough to catch Feb's gaze. "I figured you'd get a laugh seeing it from whatever monitor you were watching on with Holt. Not that you'd actually be here."

Feb smartly dodged their question and threw one back at them instead. "When's the last time you slept?" She framed Jax's cheeks, thumbs coasting under their eyes. "You look more tired than Brax, and I didn't think that was possible."

They chuckled. "I slept, usually a couple hours each morning before Sugar and Spice woke me."

She arched a brow.

"Ariel's cats. I think you'd like him. Don't tell Hawes, but he'd probably make a better sous-chef."

"You know they have a name for this? It's called Stockholm syndrome."

"Except I don't think Ariel is actually a bad guy."

Seeming to accept their rendezvous was over, Feb sighed and scooted back on the stool. "We sorted that on our end too."

"Our end?" Jax said, leaning a hip against the nook's counter.

"I'll be fine tonight," Feb said, dodging again. She was picking up Madigan maneuvers fast. "Hawes is back here."

"So is Chloe."

"Declawed," she said with a hiss, hands held up, fingers bent. "Helena made sure of that."

Jax could only imagine and chuckled again. "Would've liked to see that."

"Highlight of my year, and it's only February."

Jax shot her a side-eye, and Feb's own eye roll was epic, the both of them laughing, until Feb snuck an arm around their waist and drew them back in for a softer, less hurried brush of the lips. "Softball, I know."

Jax smirked against her lips. "I'd like to give you another highlight after we're done tonight if your date invite is still open."

Feb hesitated, slow to draw back and lift her gaze to Jax, and when she did, the earlier determination was gone, clouded with uncertainty that twisted Jax's gut. "I—"

"It's showtime," Hawes said, leaning his head into the nook.

Given the out, Feb slid off the stool and left her sentence —Jax's future—hanging.

———

Unlike Valentine's Day when it was only one person per table at UTT, tonight was supposed to be a regular Friday service with tables full of various size groups. Or at least that was how it needed to appear to whomever walked through that door looking for Ariel Camino. From their position behind the bar, Jax thought, *So far, so good*. From outside the plate glass window, it would look like a packed house, full of lively diners enjoying their drinks and food. Which most of the diners were, even if they were operatives, hunters, and LEOs, most in disguise in case tonight's visitor had had eyes on V-day or might recognize any of the "guests." In any event, whoever their target was would be outnumbered the minute they stepped through the door.

Feb, one of the few people not in disguise, shuttled dishes between the kitchen and dining room. At the moment, she stood beside the table with one of Jax's Redemption colleagues, Lette, and Lette's roommate, Special Agent Lauren Hall, aka Hacker Barbie in Holt's book of code names, and she'd played into it tonight, absolutely owning the blond wig she wore. Feb had just delivered their mains and was chatting them up like she normally would on her evening rounds.

And Jax would normally be bringing her a shot of whiskey right now. That was the image they were supposed to project tonight—business as usual—but what did Feb want, in this moment and after service was over? Jax wasn't sure about the latter after Feb's earlier hesitation in the chef's nook, but as to the former, Jax had worked with Feb long enough to know she thrived on routine. And she'd need that steadiness tonight. They grabbed Feb's favorite rye off the backbar and a tumbler.

Beside them, Avery, Helena's second in command, was mixing up cocktails for Mel and Chris. "She'll be fine," Avery said with a jut of her chin toward Feb. "She handles a knife every day. Helena just had to show her how to chuck it." She capped two shakers, shook them, then, with a smooth flick of her index fingers, ditched the lids and poured the mixtures into the prepared glasses—a paloma for Mel, a Kentucky sidecar for Chris.

"Helena teach you how to sling drinks too?"

"Nah, that's just what happens when we have to fend

for ourselves." A wink tossed over her shoulder, she picked up the tray of cocktails and sashayed out from behind the bar.

With her wild halo of curls pulled into a severe bun and her leather toned down in a less deadly, more sexy dress version, Avery looked more like a runway model tonight than an assassin, one who Jax knew had had an even rougher upbringing than them. But like with them, the Madigans had taken Avery in and made her family. And their family kept growing, Perri's and Talley's too. Maybe a Winters somewhere down the line, Jax idly—hopefully— thought as they grabbed two bottles of Gravity Stout and a pair of frosty pilsners from the under-bar fridge. They set them on the tray with Feb's whiskey, then headed out from behind the bar.

They were halfway to Lauren and Lette's table when Holt radioed, "Ariel two blocks out."

Definitely a good time to put Feb at ease. They slid in next to the chef at the side of the table. "Everyone good here?"

"You're gonna bring Feb around after this is all over, yeah?" Lette asked as Jax set their glasses and beer bottles on the table. "She can hang."

"I normally tell her to butt out," Lauren said with a flick of her hot pink nails. She leaned toward Feb and in a conspiratorial whisper added, "Lette tends to mother hen. Runs in the family. Her brothers are *the worst*. But in this case, I agree. You're cool. Please come hang with us."

Feb laughed, charmed, as most folks were by the two best friends, Lette's sweetness a perfect counter to Lauren's snark, but when Feb's gaze caught Jax's over the whiskey glass, they heated like they had in the nook, giving Jax more hope. Maybe her hesitation had been about something else.

Hope and answers, though, would have to wait, a gust of the wintery-for-San-Francisco air heralding Ariel's entrance. Jax tucked the drink tray under their arm and rested their hand at the small of Feb's back, giving it the double-tap signal for *time to go.*

"I better get back to the kitchen," she told Lauren and Lette. "But yes, I'd love to hang when this is all over."

Jax walked her to the espresso station in the breezeway, hand remaining at the small of her back, enjoying the fit there. "I'll take care of everything out here."

Feb glanced over her shoulder, heat still smoldering in her gaze. "Take care of you too."

Jax nodded, and Feb continued down the breezeway, passing Hawes striding the opposite direction. Jax waited at the edge of the dining room, then accompanied him to greet Ariel. Hawes showed him to his table, slipping him a comm device inside the menu, while Jax prepared the Manhattan he ordered. It wasn't until they delivered the drink that they noticed the gold band Ariel usually kept in his wallet on his left ring finger. By the sharp inhale over the comm, Fletcher, in the van with Holt, glimpsed it too. "Can I get you anything else?" Jax asked.

He spun the ring around his finger. "The lost years of my life back?"

"Only you can do that." They nudged the Manhattan closer. "This might help in the meantime."

"And whatever curry I'm smelling from the back."

"I'll make sure Feb gives you extra."

And she did, of everything. The roasted chickpeas, the sesame and persimmon salad, the morel and pasta midcourse, each of which Ariel raved about, asking Hawes to tell Feb she had more than earned his Render review. Her "fuck yeah" over the comms when Hawes relayed the message made Jax and the entire dining room, including Ariel, smile. It was a shame he only managed two bites of the red chicken curry before Holt radioed, "Bogey incoming. Male, midfifties, six-two, two-twenty, dark hair."

"That doesn't sound like Fitzpatrick," Jax said.

"We're running facial."

Ariel the foodie vanished, replaced with the professional, straightening in his chair and angling toward the door, knife within reach.

The door opened, the stranger—not Fitzpatrick—entering, but judging by the jolt Ariel tried and failed to suppress, the target wasn't a stranger to him. Mixing a drink, Jax lowered their chin and spoke low. "That's not Fitzpatrick. Ariel knows this person."

The man didn't wait for Hawes to reach the host stand. He walked straight to Ariel's table, pulled out the chair, and sat across from him.

"What are you doing here?" Ariel asked.

"It's what you want, isn't it? The message in your Render review was pretty clear."

"Yes, but why you?"

"Because maybe you'll listen to me before you make a terrible mistake. Your family wants—"

Ariel shot to his feet. "How do you know what my family wants?"

"Fuck, that was his CIA boss. Officer—" The bang of the surveillance van door cut off Holt's words. "Fletcher! Wait! Fuck!" The door slammed closed, then Holt was back on the line. "That's Officer Damian Barbas, and this is about to go sideways. Hawes, secure Feb."

Jax forced themselves to ignore the scramble in the van and now in the kitchen and listened closely to the scramble playing out at the table on the other side of the bar from them. Ariel was on his feet, squaring off against Damian. "I repeat," Ariel said. "What do you—"

"Ariel," the other man said, calm and stern. "Lower your voice and sit down." He aimed his gaze directly at Ariel's chair, effectively repeating the order. "You're drawing attention. I taught you better than that."

Good, Barbas didn't seem to realize the onlookers at neighboring tables were more than casual observers. Either Ariel recognized that too or the lure of answers, the opportunity to clear his name, was too powerful to resist. He lowered himself back into his seat. "Was Fitzpatrick tailing me on your orders?"

"Not mine. Your family's."

He leaned forward and braced his forearms on the table. "And back to my original question: How the fuck do you know what they want?"

"They want you back. I vouched for you."

"So you're on their payroll too?"

"I'm not that dumb." He stole Ariel's wineglass, sipping as he settled back in the chair, legs crossed. "But there is a payday waiting for me, and you're the ticket to getting it."

"I gave up everything to bring them down. We spent years cutting them off. We were a team. And now you're doing their dirty work?"

"Not the dirty part. I'm the bring-you-in-peacefully part. The other part, that would be when things get dirty."

"We've got movement outside," Holt reported. "Four bogeys converging. Talley, move your teams in."

"Move to intercept," Special Agent in Charge Aidan Talley radioed to his perimeter teams outside.

"Ariel," Jax said; the team agreed they'd be the contact with him, given the trust they'd established with Ariel the past few days. "Wrap this up."

"Did you sell me out?" he asked Barbas. "With the info Fitzpatrick provided?"

"I might have connected the dots for the higher ups at the Agency. Sold them a story about how you weren't cutting off your family's most lucrative ventures." He finished Ariel's wine, then tilted the glass toward his protégé. "You were avoiding those intentionally."

"The only thing that was intentional was building a better case, like *you* told me to do."

"But you didn't do the other thing I told you, did you?" He glared daggers at the ring on Ariel's left hand. "You just couldn't leave him alone."

As if his statement warranted an exclamation mark, gunfire erupted outside.

Barbas's gaze whipped from Ariel to the street outside the plate glass window, then back to Ariel, who broke into a grin. "Thanks for clearing my name, traitor."

Barbas bolted out of his seat, the chair falling behind him. He stumbled back, nearly falling in his haste to flee, only to find himself hemmed in, everyone else in the restaurant now on their feet, in position and blocking his path to the door. Wide-eyed, he whipped back around to Ariel. "What's going on?"

"Bogeys contained outside," Holt radioed.

Inside, Mel stepped forward. "Target is contained inside as well."

"Nowhere to run, Damian," Ariel said as Fletcher and Agent Talley strolled out from the breezeway, Feb on their heels.

Fletcher sidled to his ex-husband's side and laced his fingers with Ariel's. "You want to do the honors, Agent Talley?"

Aidan circled behind the team's true target and produced a pair of cuffs. "Damian Barbas, you're under arrest. You have the right—"

"Fletcher?" Feb interrupted. She'd stopped halfway between the breezeway and the end of the bar where Jax stood. Head tilted, topknot bobbing, a confused expression streaked across her face. "There's a red spot on your back. How did you get curry there?"

Jax whipped their gaze back to Fletcher.

Not curry.

The dot from a rifle's laser sight.

Jax dove in Feb's direction. "Sniper—get down!"

NINE

Feb stood in front of the bar, watching the blue and red lights of the patrol car outside bounce off the freshly painted walls and good-as-new shiplap ceiling. Both still intact, as with all but one of the plate glass windows. A moment later, the patrol car pulled away from the curb, its lights fading as it turned the corner, the street falling back into nighttime darkness but for the streetlights and the stand-up shop light Hawes and Holt had on the shattered window they were boarding up from the outside.

Reality seemed not, everything unreal—the events of this evening, the events of the past week—but Feb was still standing and so was her restaurant, the lights burning bright inside. Though it was noticeably less crowded than it had been a few hours ago, only Hawes and Holt outside, Jax in the kitchen, and Mel and Brax striding back inside from the cold. Feb would also like February to go back to normal San Francisco temps.

"Well, all in all," Mel said as she and Brax wove through

tables, "one broken window and a single bullet hole isn't too much to fix over the weekend."

Feb fingered the hole in the front edge of the bar. "I might leave this. Gives the place some character."

Chuckling, Brax leaned against the barstool beside her. "This place is full of character already." His gaze took a lap around the interior before landing back on her. "Really, Feb, it's a great place you've got here, and the food is dynamite."

"You know already Ariel said the same," Jax added as they emerged from the breezeway.

"How is he?" Feb asked. "And Fletcher?" She'd been hiding in the dry goods pantry like Hawes had told her to when Fletcher had barreled in through the back door—right into Hawes's chokehold. He'd halted Fletcher's forward motion in a flurry of quick, efficient maneuvers, until something over the in-ear comms had caused Hawes to loosen his hold on the struggling detective. Fletcher had shot out of his arms like he hadn't been stopped at all. He'd sprinted up the breezeway to the dining room, Hawes behind him, Feb behind Hawes.

Only it hadn't been over.

"Fletcher's fine," Brax said. "Just some bumps and bruises. The gunshot wound to Ariel's shoulder was a through and through. Docs are more concerned with the head injury he got from tackling Fletcher to the floor. They've medically induced a coma."

Feb coasted a hand over her own head, grateful Jax had taken them down on their hips, an arm around her head to cushion their fall. "I'd like to go by tomorrow. Check on them."

"I'll go with you," Jax said, then to Mel, "Do we know who the shooter was?"

She shook her head. "Camino redundancy, likely."

"We found an empty sniper's nest in the under-construction building across the square," Brax added. "Been there a while. Probably on Tuesday too."

"The both of you," Mel said, splitting a glance between her and Jax, "probably saved Ariel's life *twice*. Fletcher's too." Then to Feb, hand outstretched, commended her. "You handled all of this remarkably well, Ms. Winters."

She rolled her eyes, even as she shook the boss lady's hand. "I don't know if I'd go *that* far."

"I would," Mel said with a smile. "There's a spot for you at Redemption if you ever want it."

Feb couldn't catch the giggle that escaped. Or the truth. "No thank you. And no offense. You all are amazing, but I am not nearly as cool, and I have a three-star kitchen to run." She blew a flyaway off her forehead. "That's enough stress."

"None taken," Mel said. "And fair enough. I, for one, cannot wait to bring Danny here. He's gonna love it."

"There'll be a table waiting for you." Feb was curious as hell to meet the person who'd swept the powerhouse off her feet and somehow kept up with her.

When Brax held out his hand for a shake too, Feb walked into his arms instead, hugging him around the waist. He hugged her back, every bit the father figure she'd first taken him for. Had been through all this. "We'll finish boarding up that window tonight," he said as he drew back. "We'll be back tomorrow to take down the surveillance and reprogram the locks, then on Sunday with the new glass."

"Sounds good. Thank you for everything."

"Jax," he said, turning to them next. "Good job on point."

"HQ tomorrow?"

"Monday," Mel said. "Take the weekend off."

"It's no—"

"Monday," Brax seconded, and that was that, apparently, the two bosses headed back out the front door, the both of them so different but a perfect complement to each other.

"So, that's Mom and Dad . . ." Feb said, unable to hold in any longer the observation she'd kept bottled up for days.

"Frighteningly accurate," Jax said, chuckling as they scooted behind the bar. "Whiskey?"

Feb climbed onto a stool. "Fuck yes."

Jax worked as effortlessly behind the bar as they had since they'd first stepped behind it. Sure, it wasn't rocket science, pouring whiskey into a glass, but the flick of their wrists as they turned up two glasses, then the bottle, the drop of water they put into each whiskey to open the rye up was its own sort of science. Their movements behind the bar were practiced, like they were as suited to it as they were to computers and whatever else they did for Redemption.

But selfishly, Feb liked them behind her bar a lot better.

"I can coordinate the repairs here this weekend," they said as they slid a tumbler across the bar to her. "Then I'll be out of your hair."

Feb paused, glass halfway to her lips. "Why would you do that? I negotiated to keep you on until I can fill the spot."

Jax's green eyes widened. "You did?"

"Of course I did." She raised her glass and waited for Jax to clink their rim against it. "And I thought I negotiated a date with you . . ."

"But the stress—"

She grinned behind the rim of her glass. "Pretty sure you'll help relieve some of that."

Reaching a hand across the bar, Jax wrapped it gently around her wrist and tugged down the glass. "Feb, are you sure? You've gotten an up-close view of my life, my family—"

"I've gotten an up-close view of how devoted you are to one another and to doing right by folks you barely know." Feb covered Jax's hand with her free one and squeezed. "I'm not asking for forever yet. A date tomorrow night, and if that goes well, maybe more, but let's just worry about tomorrow night for now."

The corner of Jax's lips twitched. "Not tonight?"

"No, that was what I was going to say earlier in the nook before Hawes interrupted. We both need sleep tonight." She set her glass down, then, forearms on the bar, levered herself up and brushed her lips over Jax's. "So we can not tomorrow night."

Jax's lips curved against hers. "I like the way you think, Chef Winters."

———

Feb stepped outside her home, phone in hand to monitor the car on its way to pick her up, when Helena's sleek, roaring black SUV pulled to the curb. Boss lady was behind the wheel, her wife leaning out the passenger window with a kind, warm smile. "Hop in, Feb," Celia said. "We'll give you a lift."

"I don't think this is how it's supposed to work," Feb said, even as she climbed into the back seat. "I asked Jax out. I'm supposed to pick them up."

Helena cackled. "I can't believe you just said *supposed to* anything after the week you had." She gunned it, slinging Feb back into the seat and earning a playful backhand and "Behave" from Celia.

"She's not wrong," Feb admitted as she cancelled her car request. "Expect the unexpected, right?"

Helena snickered. "Remember you said that."

"Spoilers!" Celia hissed.

"Spoilers for what?" Feb said, leaning forward. She was well and truly intrigued, and after the last week, after the somber visit earlier today she and Jax had made to Fletcher and a still unconscious Ariel at the hospital, things could only improve.

Unfortunately, Celia wasn't playing along, changing the subject to first baked goods, then Lily, the conversation carrying the rest of the way to . . . Under the Table.

They pulled in front of Feb's restaurant, with both its windows fixed, and a sidewalk full of people—Jax's family she'd met the past week, plus chefs from her old restaurant in the city, from UTT, from Diamond, including Justin and Amanda, and others from the community. And in front of the gathering stood Jax, dressed in a sharp three-piece suit, the tie between their jacket's lapels plastered with . . . stars. "What's going on?" Feb said as Jax stepped toward the door.

Helena's smile when she looked back over her shoulder was as warm and genuine as her wife's always was. It melted the ice completely. "The celebration you deserve."

Jax opened the back door and offered her a hand. "Chef."

"What happened to date night?" she whispered low.

Jax grinned. "We'll get there, promise. But there's something everyone wanted you to see first." They lifted their chin and the crowd parted.

Beside the door, inset in stone between the doorframe and window, was a new plaque etched with three stars and the Render logo. Tears filled Feb's eyes, the stars seeming to swim, same as her insides. She knew what Ariel had said, but . . . "Is this for real?"

Jax wrapped an arm around her waist, holding her steady. "You earned it, babe."

"How?" she squeaked out. "Does it count? And so fast?"

"It counts, and don't ask those questions."

She chuckled, the sound watery from the tears clogging her throat too. "I don't wanna know."

"Now she's learning," Helena said as she and Celia joined them on the sidewalk, then led the crowd in a rousing "Happy Birthday" to Feb before leading everyone inside to party.

And a good party it was—music turned up, trays of North Carolina barbecue and sides courtesy of a still too-hot-for-this-world Jamie, and an entire mistletoe cannoli birthday cake from Angelica's Bakery. Feb made the rounds among her chefs, making sure they all knew those stars were as much theirs as hers, thanking all the other chefs there who had guided and supported her, and reintroducing everyone to Jax and to their family, who she suspected they'd be seeing a lot of at UTT in the future. But her favorite sight of the party was Jax behind the bar, at home there, filling champagne glasses for toasts and slinging drinks with Mo and guest bartender Avery.

Though after two hours, Feb's favorite sight was fast becoming the most frustrating one, a bar and way too many people between her and Jax. The bar she could work with; the people less so.

Same as she'd magically appeared with her car at the curb earlier, Helena appeared at her side now, throwing an arm over her shoulders. "You ready for your date now?"

"Fuck yeah."

"Fantastic." Then she stuck two fingers between her lips and let out a piercing whistle that had everyone's head turning their direction. "All righty, folks," she said, voice raised. "Party's not over, but Feb and Jax have a private party to get to."

More whistles and catcalls filled the air, and Feb's cheeks burned. Even Jax's were a little pink as they ducked out from behind the bar and crossed to where she stood with Helena. "I thought you were gonna make me wait all night."

"Was just waiting for the all clear," Helena said.

"What all clear?" Jax replied at the same time as Feb's, "That sounds ominous."

"It's good," Helena said with a wink as she held the door open. "Promise."

Feb paused over the threshold and asked the only question that really mattered. "Is it private?"

"Oh yeah."

Feb grabbed Jax's hand and tugged them toward the SUV waiting at the curb again. "Let's fucking go." She was done waiting.

———

"What is this place?"

Feb made a slow circle where she stood in the center of an unfamiliar South Beach condo, trying to process everything her eyes were taking in. A wall of windows that overlooked a winter green courtyard, easels and canvases leaned against the walls of the open-plan living area, a bottle of whiskey and two tumblers on the kitchen bar, and twinkling fairy lights draped from one end of the space to a loft bedroom above the kitchen at the other end. "Do you live here?"

"God no," Jax scoffed, then pointed toward the floor. "A bit too close to the office." They undid their tie and tossed it and their jacket on the sectional that separated the kitchen area from the rest of the . . . studio space? "It's an artist's loft," they confirmed as they headed for the kitchen. "The Madigans used to own it when the unit below was Hawes's. Now Mel and Danny own it since Hawes's old unit was converted to Redemption HQ." Jax peeled open the whiskey bottle and poured them each a shot. "Technically, Mel and Danny own the entire building, but we only occupy these two units. If there's no one renting up here, we use it as a crash pad when operations run long or when we need more space to chill out."

Feb could see that, the Zen of the place no doubt a

welcome—necessary—escape from the high-stress work Jax and their colleagues handled. After witnessing a small slice of it the past week, Feb appreciated that the Redemption folks had a place like this. As long as that escape wasn't tonight, because she was out of appreciation for interruptions. "How do we know no one will barge in on us?"

Jax smiled as they circled around the sectional and handed her a whiskey. "Because as soon as I figured out where we were headed, I reset the lock code from my phone."

"God, you're sexy."

"Competence kink," Jax said with a wink. "Noted."

Feb tossed back her whiskey, then set her glass aside. Eyeing Jax, she couldn't help but think she really wished they had left their tie on. As it was, she settled, not unhappily, with her hands on Jax's hips, drawing them closer. "I have some other notes for you."

"I'm all ears."

"I like you in suits." She popped a button on Jax's vest and took a step forward, forcing Jax a step back. "I like you in leather." Another button, another step. "I like you in button-downs and funny ties." The last button, the last step before the backs of Jax's legs bumped into the sectional. "I like everything about you, Jax Dillon." Jax opened their mouth as if to object, and Feb gave them a playful shove, enough to send them toppling back onto the couch. "Even your family," she said as she followed them down, her knees on either side of Jax's hips. "They're pretty awesome, like you."

Determined to attack their shirt buttons next, Feb lifted her hands to get started, but Jax intercepted her, clasping her hands in their own and holding them against their chest. "I like you too, Feb. A lot." Sensing a *but* or caveat in their tone, Feb lifted her gaze and saw a not small amount of guilt swirling in Jax's eyes. "And I'm sorry I lied to you," they said. "About who I was and what we were doing at UTT. I should have told you sooner. I needed to say that before this goes any further."

Relief flooded through Feb, propelled her to erase the distance to the lips she'd wanted to claim all night. No more buts, no more hesitation. And Jax didn't hesitate to return the kiss either, the last of their walls coming down, their arms circling Feb's shoulders and hauling her down on top of them as they fell back against the cushions. Laughing, something Jax had always been good at getting her to do.

Feb braced a hand in the cushion, taking in the gorgeous being beneath her, who, despite an alias and a job to do, was the same good, smart, creative, helpful person when it counted, when Feb had needed them most. "If you hadn't been at UTT," she said, "I might not have gotten my three stars, so let's call it even."

Jax reached up, pushing a strand of hair back behind her ear. "You would have." Then pulling the elastic out altogether. "You're that fucking talented, February Winters."

"I'd like to show you how talented." She lifted a hand to Jax's open collar, determined to pick up where she'd left off before, then stopped herself short; she needed to ask something before they went any further. "I need to know if there are any parts of your body you want me to pay more or less attention to?"

"You're good," Jax said with a soft smile. "I don't experience dysphoria, but thank you for asking. I just don't feel like I fit into either the man or woman box our society seems so keen to put us in. Nonbinary feels more comfortable for me, like I can express the me I am, honestly, on any given day."

"Well, I'm keen on you every day." Feb smirked and, by Jax's answering laugh, figured it didn't come off nearly as sexy as she meant it to, but she didn't care because to hear the person she'd been falling for the past three months, could see falling for forever, sound so free was better than she could have imagined.

The laughter tasted even better, Feb capturing Jax's mouth with hers again, keeping it occupied, no more interruptions, as she worked free the buttons of their dress shirt and pushed it open, along with the vest still hanging unbuttoned.

"You happy now?" Jax said. "Buttons undone, finally."

"Not completely," she replied with a waggle of her brows before dipping down and blowing a raspberry against their neck, bringing out more of that laughter she couldn't get enough of. Jax let her get away with it two more times—the other side of their neck, the hollow of their throat—before the training Feb had only seen in brief flashes asserted itself, Jax flipping their positions so Feb was laid out on the couch beneath them.

They coasted their lips down Feb's throat, making Feb groan and arch her neck for more. "I really don't think there's anything wintery about you, Ms. Winters." A hand slid between her thighs, cupping her through the dressiest pair of yoga pants she'd been able to find in her closet tonight. "Definitely seems like summer down here." Pressed harder, no doubt feeling the wetness beginning to gather there. "Pool weather."

Feb scoffed at the bad joke, then made a bad one of her

own. "You wouldn't know anything about that, would you? Born and raised in San Francisco."

They cracked up laughing at the same time, continued laughing as they rid each other of their clothes, as they levered up, limbs tangled, long enough to yank the blanket off the back of the couch onto the cushions, then fell back on it, lips curved against each other's. "Tell me what you want, Feb," Jax whispered.

"For this not to be the only time." The words were out before she could catch them, and she thought for a moment that maybe she'd given away too much, but then Jax's green gaze turned from hot to boiling.

"Oh, baby," they practically purred. "I plan for this to be the first time of many." They cupped her breast and flicked their thumb over her nipple. "Countless, if I have my way."

Feb liked the sound of *countless*. Liked the feel of it around her nipple, Jax repeating the word as they mimicked the motion of their thumb with their tongue on her other breast. "Fuck yeah," Feb groaned, rocking her hips, chasing friction where her blood was racing, her clit throbbing with each flick of Jax's tongue. She'd need count-less at the rate this time was speeding along. She'd need all the chances to get to know Jax's body too, the little glimpses she was getting only hints—the way their pale skin turned rosy, the way they shivered at a hand coasted down their side, the way they growled at fingers digging into their ass. The gasp they gave when Feb shifted so her thigh collided with their center. They ground against it, the heat and wetness searing Feb. "Fuck," Feb cursed again. "You're close too."

"I had plans," Jax groaned as they rocked again. "To torture you all night long."

Feb drew back enough to meet their lust-clouded gaze. "Aren't you glad I sent you home to sleep last night?"

More laughter, and a smack to the thigh for the sass. "You'll pay for that."

"I hope so."

"Before I haul you up and make us both come, you tested recently?"

"Negative."

"Negative," they echoed. "Let's get one in the books, then." They smirked. "I owe the three-star chef at least three orgasms tonight."

"Seems fa—" Feb's cheeky reply was cut off by another flurry of Jax's precise movements. Lifting Feb up like they'd promised, shifting them, then angling their bodies together where they were both aching for friction.

Jax's usually precise words weren't so exact after that. Neither were Feb's. Moans littered with curses as they rocked and shifted, rubbed together, until Feb couldn't hold out any longer. "Jax, please," she keened.

"Let go, Feb," they said, tangling their fingers together. "Let go with me."

As her orgasm washed over her, as Jax gathered her into their arms after, Feb thought countless might not be nearly enough.

———

For all the latest updates on new projects, sneak peeks, and more, including what's next for Redemption Inc., sign up for Layla's Newsletter.

———

Reviews are an invaluable tool when it comes to spreading the word about great reads. Please consider leaving an honest review for *The Accidental* on your favorite review site.

Thank you for reading!

ACKNOWLEDGMENTS

From a farm's worth of plot bunnies, Allison Temple and I originally enlisted some author friends for the multi-author series, Accidentally Undercover, where this story first appeared as *Under the Table*.

I was so excited to tell fan-favorite Jax's story and to combine my two great genre loves: romantic suspense and foodie romance. I'm doubly excited to re-release Jax and Feb's story as *The Accidental*, a prequel novella in the long-awaited *Redemption Inc.* series. Stay tuned for more bounty hunter and hacker madness!

Shout-outs to Kelley York at Sleepy Fox Studio for the brilliant cover, to Adam Mongaya and Lori Parks on editing, to Kim on the beta read, to Kate on graphics, and to the Fairy Plot Mother for the marketing assistance.

Finally, a raised glass to everyone who clamored for Jax's story over the years. Your love and support of them and me made this book possible!

ALSO BY LAYLA REYNE

For the most up-to-date list of titles and a helpful reading order, please visit www.laylareyne.com.

Agents Irish and Whiskey:

Single Malt

Cask Strength

Barrel Proof

Tequila Sunrise

Blended Whiskey

Angel's Share

Trouble Brewing:

Imperial Stout

Craft Brew

Noble Hops

Final Gravity

Fog City:

Prince of Killers

King Slayer

A New Empire

Queen's Ransom

Silent Knight

Perfect Play:

Dead Draw

Bad Bishop

King Hunt

Best Play

Redemption Inc:

The Accidental

The Bounty

The Martyr

The Boss

More Romantic Suspense / Mystery:

What We May Be

Variable Onset

Soul to Find:

Icarus and the Devil

Jason and the Storm

Paris and the Reaper

Atlas and the Traitor

Table for Two:

The Last Drop

Dine With Me

Blue Plate Special

Over a Barrel

The Sweet Spot

Sigh of Relief

Changing Lanes:

Relay

Medley

Freestyle

More Contemporary Romance:

Barn Burner

Eyes on You

ABOUT THE AUTHOR

Layla Reyne is the author of *What We May Be* and the *Agents Irish and Whiskey, Fog City,* and *Perfect Play* series. She writes sexy, intense LGBTQIA+ romance featuring competent adults in kitchens, sports arenas, car chases, and other high-stakes situations. Whether it's adrenaline-fueled suspense, rival athletes, vampires and shifters, or love mixed with mouth-watering foodie goodness, queer folks finding happily-ever-afters is guaranteed.

You can find Layla online at laylareyne.com and at the following sites:

BB bookbub.com/authors/layla-reyne

f facebook.com/laylareyne

instagram.com/laylareyne

tiktok.com/@laylareyne

bsky.app/profile/laylareyne